The Thirteenth Crime

Rocket Science Press
SHIPWRECKT BOOKS PUBLISHING COMPANY
Winona, Minnesota

The Thirteenth Crime

The Ghosts of Injustice in Frontier Otter Tail County

Janet Preus

Cover and interior design by Shipwreckt Books
Cover photo of Otter Tail County, Minnesota, by Janet Preus

Shipwreckt Books Publishing Company
357 W. Wabasha Street
Winona, Minnesota 55987

Library of Congress Control Number: 2024941329

To Tim Andersen, who read every page of every
revision of this book.

Contents

THE SETUP

Part 1. GETTING AWAY WITH MURDER

THE OUTCOME

THE SETUP

The May night in 1996 I visited the site of Lillie Field's murder, it was pleasant. A teaching colleague, his son and my daughter, both teens, came along. The waning moon provided some half-light, and our feet rustled along the top of the embankment where a fence line reminded us that these woods belonged to someone. Otherwise, it was as if it had been left to Lillie herself—untouched, it appeared, since the farm was abandoned decades ago. We sat and waited for Lillie's ghost, a specter in white, to appear. She didn't, and eventually we retraced our way back to my Chevy Blazer, but I was still thinking about Lillie. I had nothing to do with this young girl from more than a century back. She wasn't my family, but that didn't seem to matter to her; she had my attention, and she wasn't letting go.

"This must be the way ghosts operate," I thought, "Invading our consciousness and just staying there."

Ghosts. Plural. There were more spirits circling the dark corners of Otter Tail County's past, and the list grew. Persistent though she was, Lillie would have to wait. Surely all ghosts want their stories told,

1

especially those who left this earth without the satisfaction of a just conclusion.

Lillie and I would like you to know that all the substantive historical information in this book is factual. There are embellishments, but I have taken great care to be faithful to the facts as I know them. Feel free to decide for yourself the role that Lillie, or any other ghosts, may have played in telling these stories.

Part I covers the crimes leading up to Lillie's murder. I think it explains a great deal about Lillie's case, which is Part II. You will also see narrative, such as what you are now reading, that's indented and on a light grey background. This indicates "setup" for individual crimes, as well as the Lillie Field case. This formatting tells you the section offers more background, my interpretations, conclusions I've drawn, and theory based on much more research than I could include. These narratives are found at the beginning of Part I and Part II, the beginning of each chapter in Part I, and the end of some chapters in Part I. All of the Epilogue is also my commentary on Nels Holong's defense and his fate, specifically. It is, however, impossible to separate out all the larger questions about "justice," and that's why there's a book.

Janet Preus, January 2025

Part 1. GETTING AWAY WITH MURDER

Thirteen crimes including seven unpunished murders culminated in Otter Tail County's first legal hanging—the case of Lillie Field's murder. It was sensational news across Minnesota, given the horrific details of the killing, but there was another reason: Nels Holong was not the only one on trial. Otter Tail County had never punished a murderer.

County Attorney Lewis made a strong speech and in closing asked the jury to render a verdict such as would insure [sic] the safety of our homes and to retrieve the good name of Otter Tail County from the odium which had been fastened upon it for its unpunished crimes. —Fergus Falls *Weekly Journal, November 24, 1887.*

County Attorney Lewis opened the case for the state. ... He called the attention of the jury to the fact that no murderer had ever been convicted in this county and that it was a by-word throughout the state ... A shudder of horror crept over each one as the tale passed from hand to hand and everyone seemed to vow in silence that this, the eight (sic) and most bloody murder in Otter Tail County should not like the other seven go unpunished. Until the conviction of Holong a murder had never been punished in Otter Tail County, and it had been the scene of many a bloody and cruel one, and on many instances there had been no doubt as to the guilty ones.
— Fergus Falls *Weekly Journal,* April 19, 1888

The county was going to have to reckon with its past failures and exonerate itself for a list of crimes so commonly known in 1887 that the Fergus Falls *Weekly Journal,* reporting on the trial (in 1888), didn't even have to name them. Who were these seven killers, and why was Nels Holong the one to bring this "odium" to an end? [i]

1. Thieves, Thugs and Murderers, July 1871

*I*t is twenty-six years since the first locomotive awoke the primeval solitudes in northern Minnesota. Up to 1870 the great valley of the Red River and its tributaries had been a wilderness, uninhabited save by Scotch and French half-breeds and Indians. But the time had come when a new era was to be ushered in. The Yankee spirit of enterprise was about to travel westward ... There was a strange, cosmopolitan population, including many human beings given up to vice. I had a good opportunity to see this motley throng, and after the lapse of twenty-six years, I am convinced that a larger assortment of bad men, thieves, thugs, murderers, adventurers and abandoned women were assembled on that beautiful lake [Otter Tail] than have ever since infested a new town in Minnesota. ... There were many good people there, too, but Satan was there also. ... The condition of society in that period in Otter Tail City can be but faintly imagined, but I wish it kept in mind [concerning] the circumstances of a terrible tragedy. —Fergus Falls *Weekly Journal*, June 3, 1897, for the Minneapolis *Times* by George C. Whitcomb, Surveyor.

The first reported murder was a "supposed murder." There was overwhelming evidence of a crime, the victim known and the perpetrators obvious enough. But in the dense, hilly forests on the fringes of the county, far from what little law enforcement existed, the killers could melt into the semi-wilderness, dispose of the evidence, and make their way to the even less established Dakota Territories, if they wished, with little fear of apprehension. More to the point, the body was never found, so the murder will remain "supposed."

The report, written by surveyor George C. Whitcomb twenty-six years after the incident, described the lawless milieu in which it happened, recounting details of the story, including his discovery of irrefutable physical evidence. But without a body, the perpetrators got away with murder.

1. A portion of the 1884 "Outline Plan of Otter Tail County, Minnesota." Start in the upper right-hand corner to find Otter Tail City. Trace a path south through Nidaros and into Leaf Mountain to follow the victim's— and the killers'—trail to Mrs. Wortzel's house.

A Gentleman with Blond Curls, Summer 1871

The little settlement of Otter Tail had sprouted into a town of about 2,000 people by 1871. Houses of lumber and canvas popped up, and tents filled in spaces in between. All manner of carts, wagons, horses, and humanity descended on the place. A gentleman of about 30 years wearing a fine suit of Scotch worsted took Stuttering Johnny's hack from the old Chippewa station west of Alexandria to Otter Tail one late June day in 1871.

It would have been hard not to notice him. Blond curls descended from under his slouch hat and matched a finely groomed, curled moustache. His hand gripped a quality, French leather portmanteau. He was an easy mark for all manner of skullduggery, Stuttering Johnny thought. Now, Johnny may have had a speech problem, but he could still handle a rough character if he had to. Trouble was, in Otter Tail City they came in larger quantities.

By nightfall on that day in June—and even well into the night—wagons, horses and riders, and people on foot were still showing up in town. The din of voices in the packed mud street, the guffaws and drunken shouting from the saloons, the horses whinnying, the oxen bawling—it took hours to settle down, and never got quiet altogether. Somewhere in all those wagons there came one carrying four men. They had a fine, new camping outfit—a rolled wall tent, sturdy iron cookware, bed rolls and the like. In the group was a man of about 50 years, well preserved, with steel gray eyes under shaggy eyebrows set wide apart. The others, all younger, called him "Dad."

The morning of June twenty-eighth was bright and clear. The four men had their tent pitched and were chatting in front of it. The gentleman with the blond curls was there, too; one of the younger men, called "Softy," had also been at the Chippewa station the day before. He was watching the well-dressed stranger carefully and went so far as to shadow him to the lake when the stranger undressed for a swim under a clump of water willows.

... One of my surveying crew saw "Softy" looking through his field glass at the stranger. The morning of the first day of July the stranger with his portmanteau in his hand and carrying a light cane, left that city of gamblers and thieves and started south on the road he had come over to get there. Within half an hour after his departure the four men with the team and the camping outfit took the same road. ... An hour later he [the stranger] was on the road crossing the Nidaros prairie. He made his way to the house of a Mrs. Wortzel, a widow woman living near the point where the road enters the Leaf mountains. Mrs. Wortzel was in the habit of keeping people overnight. ... We are indebted to W.W. Corliss Esq. of Clitheral for facts which we give below, which indicates that foul murder has been perpetrated. It appears that the man supposed to be murdered was a traveller (sic) and stopped at the house of Mrs. Weazel at the foot of Leaf Mountains on the road to Brandon, to stay overnight. —Fergus Falls *Advocate,* July 22, 1871.

Mrs. Wortzel, Early July 1871

My place is decent, I reckon. I don't butter up the bacon, but with the sorts that come 'round here that'd be a perfect waste. There are some rough ones as stay here, but I keep my shotgun loaded and handy, don't you worry.

That night before, I had five travelers come in: one on foot and the other four in a wagon. First one in the wagon said his name was "Smith." Ha! You wouldn't believe how many Mr. Smiths come out to the frontier these days. Didn't even bother to ask what the others was going to call themselves, as I figured one lie would do.

Well, this first one come in—the one missing next day. He showed up alone. Now, I can still turn a head pretty good. Not one grey hair and got all my teeth. But proper is proper, so when this dude come in like he's the biggest toad in the puddle, with his golden, waxed moustache curled up in points, and makes a remark about "half-breeds" and my "soft, brown skin," I was ready to get him out the door and let some abandoned lady in Otter Tail city deal with his fancy pants.

Funny thing, I'm more German than not. Besides, but for Indians and half-breeds, I wouldn't have made it out here without my husband. The People, as they like to call themselves, always been kind to me, especially after my husband was took in the War. I set to work puttin' some supper in front of him anyhow and I no more got it on the table then in tromps a man about my age and three more younger fellas. This older one they called "Dad," so's must've been that. He sets down to Mr. Fancy-Pants supper with not so much as a how-de-do! I says I'll fix your supper, too, but "Dad" says it was good enough for them and ran things pretty much to suit themselves from then on—even kicked my Pa out of his cot, and made that poor old man sleep on the floor when it got time for bed!

Mr. Fancy-Pants didn't have much to say for himself from that point. My poor little German girl what helps out in the kitchen and such, she's not leaving that stove for anything, standing there with a chunk 'a firewood in one hand, watching "Dad" from the other side of the stove. I thought she was going to stand there all night, but she finally scampered upstairs to her cubby.

I made up beds upstairs, but before I went to my cot in the kitchen, I saw the young guy they called "Softy" take a drink from a bottle in his pocket—or at least he made a big show of needing "a little something" to make him sleep, then offers some to Fancy-Pants, who says, "If it don't kill you; it won't hurt me," and takes a drink. Weren't long and he's dead out and snoring.

Gettin' on towards daybreak, the four men what come in that wagon together was up and at 'em. Boy, were they! Let my cattle out into the wheat, they did, so off I go to round 'em up. Took me some time, never mind the damage caused. So, when I come back, I'm wondering, 'Where did that last man go to,' as there was five of 'em last night and looked after the one what was still in bed—I thought. Didn't want no sickness hanging 'round my place, you understand. That news would travel up and down the old Woods Trail to Fort Snelling like it was a forest fire with a tail wind. So that's what I was thinking (and kind of cussin' him out to myself already, truth be told) when

I went on upstairs as the last "Mr. Smith" disappeared over the hill and passed the lake.

So, up I go and knock on the door. No answer, so I open it. Now, that was something I don't ever care to see again. Blood all over in the common room what has my beds to let. I smelled it before I saw that pool a' blood and the mess. Just a big mess. Ruined that bed, too, as it was completely soaked. But no Mr. Fancy-Pants. How all this come to pass, I don't know, but it made my heart start a'thumpin' a little faster, and I looked out the window to make sure that wagon they came in was good and gone.

All that's left in the room was a key that t'weren't mine, and buttons ripped from the man's coat. I kept the buttons, 'cause they was handmade and looked to be worth having. I don't suppose they'll ever find that body, assuming that's what he is now. That's all I know."

... Two weeks later I was camped in the Leaf mountains making a survey of the town with my surveying crew. Our camp was about half a mile north of the Otter Tail Road. In a small opening in the most secluded part of the valley I noticed an abandoned camp; horses had evidently been kept there a day or two and the party I judged, consisted of three or four men. ... The seclusion of the locality they had selected induced me to stop and look over the surroundings. ... In the rain-washed bed of ashes and coals and half-burned branches, lay the remains of a partly consumed portmanteau, or hand grip; it was made of fine French russet leather and contained a quantity of half consumed letters and the remains of several cabinet-sized portraits, one of which I had copied. Wet ashes had obliterated the others. —George Whitcomb for the Minneapolis *Times.*

2. A Quarrelsome, Dangerous Man, Christmas Eve 1874

It's a good thing for the county that he is out of the way of committing any further deeds of violence. —Perham *News*, late December 1874.

Reputable news reporting today would not print what the Perham *News* said about the first murder on the *Journal's* list of seven. They *could* say it, though, because it was what others were thinking, too. Ed Brunson was not just quarrelsome, he was dangerous—at least when he was drunk.

And he was drunk—and violent—much of the time. "Unreasonably jealous and reckless," said the Fergus Falls *Advocate*, evidenced by a previous incident when he put a gun to one Mr. McArthur's head, but first asked for a few caps from McArthur himself to fire it. When he pulled the trigger, the gun misfired, and bystanders stepped in to prevent another attempt.

Many white men married Native American women, which did not necessarily offer the women any added status; Brunson's "squaw wife" was not afforded so much as a name in the news report. Brunson lived with his wife in the house of a man named Sanders. Brunson frequently got drunk and accused Sanders of intimacy with his wife. This is hard to picture in a small cabin and under the combined noses of Sanders' wife and three children. But nobody regarded it as a credible claim, anyway, given Sanders' far more respectable persona. Brunson had also threatened to kill them all, so, true or not, the entire household could be in peril, and, given the household's remote location and distance from any law enforcement, few options were available at the moment Brunson's anger exploded.

Still, Sanders was shouldering a shotgun at close range when the final confrontation came, and he could have chosen to wound Brunson—a point not mentioned in news reports. If Sanders had shot Brunson in the leg, it might have killed him anyway, but there's another reason Sanders was exonerated with little fanfare: nobody wanted a man like Brunson around. Sanders would have been scoffed at (privately, at least) for not finishing the job when he had the chance—and the perfect pretext.

... Two weeks before the final act took place, Brunson enticed Sanders into a cellar near the house and endeavored to bring on a conflict in which he would have undoubtedly killed him had he not been near the door where he could step out of the clear, which he did and Brunson ceased. From that time he seemed on the watch for an opportunity to kill him, and there seems to be good reason to believe that had he succeeded in killing Mr. Sanders, he would have followed it up by the murder of the women and children. —Perham *News*, quoted in the Fergus Falls *Weekly Journal*, December 24, 1874

Mr. Regan, Joseph Sanders' Neighbor

Joseph Sanders might have met his end in that cellar if he hadn't been by the door, so he had a shot at escaping Brunson's threats. From then on, Sanders was convinced that Brunson meant to do him in and fasten blame upon a band of Indians encamped at Little Rabbit nearby. On the night of the cellar incident, there were some Indians who were good and drunk on a supply of whiskey gotten someplace. I'm Sander's neighbor, you see, and from what I know, it could very well have been Brunson's whiskey. "Wouldn't put it past him," I told Mr. Webster, who lives with me.

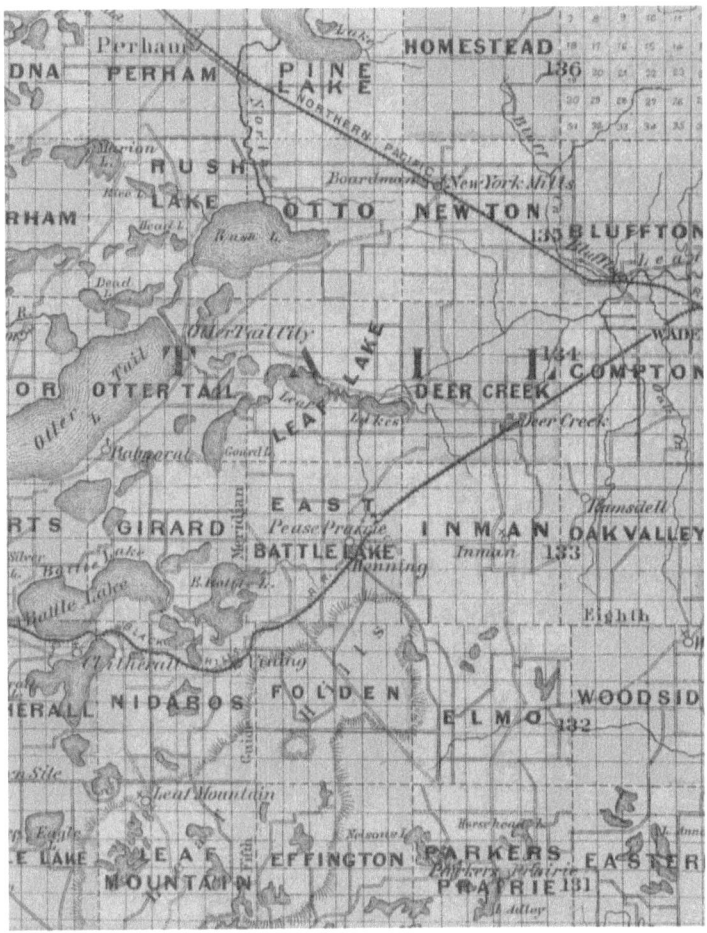

2. The 1884 "Outline Plan of Otter Tail County, Minnesota," roughly the eastern side of the county with townships referenced in the first nine chapters. The tiny village of Deer Creek held more than its share of big news in the county's early history. Map provided by the Otter Tail County Historical Society Museum.

Funny thing, Brunson worked for Sanders, who's a land agent, and he even lived in his house. Two families, under that one roof, which would've been perfectly natural, if Brunson hadn't been convinced that Sanders was having intimate relations with his squaw wife. Well, nobody believed it, a' course. But nobody was likely to cross him on it, either. Brunson was a big bear of a man with long, graying hair and a full beard. His looks, drunkenness and reckless talk were

13

enough to make sure most folks would steer clear of him. Sanders was average-sized, like me and I wouldn't 'a tangled with that Brunson, either. What was Sanders to do against a man like that?

The night Sanders shot him, Brunson was drunk and going on once again about Sanders and his wife, and he threatened to kill 'em all; Brunson's rants had become a matter of course, and, if anything, were getting worse. Sanders kept a cool head that night, though, and he crawled out his bedroom window to make a run for it to my cabin about a half mile away.

Webster was home, so he come, too, and we all go back to Sanders' house. Sanders crawled back in the bedroom window totin' Webster's double-barrel. Webster and me were a little jumpy, I don't mind sayin', but with Brunson being so drunk, we figured we could outsmart him. Damned if it wasn't Brunson who opened the door and the three of us had a pleasant chat, all nice as you please—until Sanders came in the room. That got Brunson all riled up again and he made for his shotgun in the corner. I told him to leave it be, and to my relief, he did. Sanders hot-footed it into his own room, with Brunson rushing in after him, but Sanders was ready and met him with one shot to the head. Brunson died on the spot. Didn't even have a chance to grab a knife that lay open on a table right by him.

Sanders' self-defense plea stuck well enough. The jury deliberated for all of two hours before giving up and rendering no verdict at all. A hung jury. The judge might have ordered a new trial, but he didn't, so that tells you something, I'd say. Men like Brunson are better gotten rid of. Yessir, if a man defends himself from that sort, the law should back him up.

3. The Dance of Death, April 1875

This story is so singular, tied as it is to a specific era, that sceptics might question its validity—especially given the newspapers' penchant in the 1870s for sensationalizing. But the same facts were reported by two newspapers, including the Fergus Falls *Weekly Journal*, which made the point that, had the young man lived and the girl been killed, everyone would have felt quite differently about him. His intent was clear, his plan was in place, and the execution of the plan nearly perfect; however, the young perpetrator just didn't know quite enough about a lady's undergarments.

But the story is not a quaint commentary on a bygone era to be dismissed with a chuckle. It's an example of a crime of passion gone awry—in a bizarre way, to be sure—but the attempted murder of a woman by a man who claims he loves her is a heart-wrenching story no matter what the circumstances.

An article of clothing, which was, in this case, the woman's savior, is now viewed with scorn as a relic of how women were once laced into their clothes with such ferocity that rigid stays were needed to keep all in place. At one point, stays would have been whale bone. Lucky for Maria Anderson they had progressed to something more modern–and durable.

THE DANCE OF DEATH!

A PROSPECTIVE BRIDAL ENDS IN A TOMB!

A JILTED LOVER SHOOTS AT HIS HEART'S IDOL!

CORSETS SAVE HER LIFE!

BUT HE SUCCEEDS IN KILLING HIMSELF

Last Friday evening, our hitherto quiet village was startled by the report that a tragedy had been enacted in our midst, and that a young man of promise had Rushed Into Eternity hastening to the scene of the tragedy, at Nelson's Hall, we saw stretched upon the floor, the corpse of Thomas Nelson, who but a brief half hour before had walked our streets in perfect health. —Fergus Falls *Advocate, April 28, 1875.*

In the spring of 1875, Otter Tail County was fresh with its first crop of settlers' offspring sprouted into young adulthood. Thomas Nelson was one of the lucky ones, finding, wooing and claiming as his own the charming Maria Anderson. She returned his affection, and they were engaged.

But her intended couldn't find suitable work in the area near Fergus Falls, Minnesota, where their families had settled, and so he accepted a position in Wisconsin. They wrote numerous letters over the next many months, "all breathing the same spirit of love and constancy," said the Fergus Falls *Advocate.* Except for the last letter Maria wrote to him.

She had again written Nelson that she had concluded to not fulfill her engagement with him. This letter, sent about the date of his leaving the pine woods [of Wisconsin], was never received. —Fergus Falls *Weekly Journal, May 5, 1875.*

Oblivious of her change of heart, Tom made a stop in Minneapolis to order a new suit for their upcoming wedding, arriving in Fergus Falls with a solid gold ring tucked away in

3. From the 1884 "Outline Plan of Otter Tail County, Minnesota" showing the townships as named at the time. This portion is roughly the western half of the county and includes Elizabeth, Fergus Falls, and Pelican Rapids. You'll notice that the St. Paul – Minneapolis -Manitoba rail line goes right through Fergus Falls, which explains much about how it became the county seat. Map provided by the Otter Tail County Historical Society Museum.

his pocket with $253 in cash. He was soon to discover Maria had not just broken off their engagement, she had a new beau, as well. "The serpent in the garden," the *Advocate* story called Tom's rival, but Maria's new man had not won her over entirely, and she returned to Tom's arms. She was not about to return with him to Wisconsin, however, and they quarreled.

It was a rough couple of weeks. Tom was bitterly disappointed. His pals thought he could use cheering up by holding a dance. What he needed was to take note of all the pretty girls in the area that weren't available last time he looked. It was good of them to try, and it might have worked, but they underestimated just how smitten he was with his fiancée and to what lengths he was prepared to go to settle things permanently. Nevertheless, arrangements were made and Nelson's Hall in Fergus Falls—the very property that Tom owned with another respected local, Mr. Harris—was chosen for the event.

It was a Friday night. An early snowmelt had left the streets rutted but dry. Clouds were breaking up, revealing a brilliant half-moon rising behind the riverbank where the hall was located, right in the center of town. Late April promised warmer days and young people were anxious to gather, the men in freshly pressed shirts under their Sunday best, the women in starched petticoats or bustles under cotton dresses, offering a pleasant change from their winter woolens.

The dancing was already underway when Tom showed up, alone. There she was, sitting with another young man. Even so, Tom remained a quiet spectator, altogether the reserved, sober, and decent young man known to all. He watched when at last her escort took the lovely Miss Anderson out on the dance floor.

When they returned to their seats, Tom approached. She extended her hand to him—Tom's rival made no move to stop either of them—and escorted her to a quiet corner where they could talk.

Nobody noticed the revolver stuck in his belt.

She offered to just go home if he wished.

18

"You know I cannot bear to see you here," he said, then drew the gun and fired it at the woman he claimed to love.

Maria instantly bolted to the stairway and ran down the steps. Just as quickly, Tom turned the gun on himself, fired at his chest and "sprang forward, toward the stairway nearly fifteen feet, where he fell to the floor," the *Advocate* reported.

Her escort caught up with Maria, who was dashing down the street, and took her home, where the stunned young lady discovered one of the steel stays in her corset bent, and a flattened bullet resting just under the skin behind it. It was then that she learned of the second shot and its fatal result, and "was overcome with agony."

On Saturday, an express package arrived for Mr. Nelson containing his wedding suit—arrived just in time to be his shroud. —Fergus Falls *Weekly Journal, May 7, 1875.*

In any aspect it was a mournful affair and will carry grief to the hearts of the friends of both, as well as embitter the years of the surviving actor in the tragedy. —Fergus Falls *Advocate, April 28, 1875.*

4. A Feud and a Fence, June 1878

In one of the finest tracts of timber country in Otter Tail County, not more than thirty rods apart, lived W.T. Barnes and W.S. Heathcote … Here in this lovely forest, shut out from the winds and storms of the prairie, was nursed that fire and blast of hate which has terminated in a tragic, not to say murderous assault. On the 20th day of last month, a feud of years standing, and which had involved in more or less degree nearly all the people of the town of Deer Creek culminated in the event referred to, and which has produced the death of a valuable citizen. —Fergus Falls *Weekly Journal, June 14, 1878*

Why, exactly, W.T. Barnes and W.S. Heathcote "nursed that fire and blast of hate," is not altogether clear. It had to do with a fence that provided access between their properties, but how this long-standing disagreement became a "murderous assault" is hard to figure. Even more puzzling is that Barnes' and Heathcote's argument had the residents of Deer Creek lining up on one side or another of this fence controversy. Both the victim and the perpetrator "nursed the fire," but only one had a weapon when they met late in May on the road near their homes.

On the face of it, Heathcote's acquittal for killing Barnes is a simple case of self-defense. Barnes attacked first, the accused claimed, and he thought Barnes had a gun. Heathcote had a large club, which he used to beat the victim senseless. With a self-defense plea this flimsy, Heathcote's acquittal must be attributed to other factors, and that's when the case takes on some odd kinks, not the least of which is the inexplicable action taken by Barnes' doctor:

Dr. Cromett, the attending physician, calling Dr. Mallory, of Perham, to his assistance, held a postmortem examination of the body on the day following the death, notwithstanding that the county attorney had given instructions that in case of Barnes' death an inquest must be held. As these physicians removed and carried away the brain and heart, the postmortem held under the direction of the county coroner was not so satisfactory as it would otherwise have been. —Fergus Falls *Journal,* June 14, 1878

> The brain and heart that were "carried away" never turned up again, and Barnes' gun, which Heathcote claimed Barnes had, was never found, either. The club, however, that Heathcote had used to beat Barnes *was* found—right where Heathcote had dropped it at the scene of the crime.

Sam Gordon: On The Fence

He once counted himself a friend of Heathcote's, Sam Gordon did, or a neighbor with whom he had maintained a cordial relationship at least. Sam appreciated the odd pint of whiskey Heathcote could reliably provide from his personal stash. These transactions were just between the two, to avoid the licensing nonsense hatched by the county—and the ire of Sam's wife, Frances.

"Here we are with a farm and four young 'uns. Where's the extra to spend on indulgences like drink?" she'd say. From Sam's point of view, with a farm, a wife and four young'uns, a nip of whisky was exactly the indulgence he needed.

So, when the whole fracas with Barnes and Heathcote heated up, Sam kept his opinions astride the fence, seeing no point in participating in their conflict. Prior to the assault, everyone Sam knew had lined up on one side or the other, but he just couldn't bring himself to care who did what with that damn fence, or their bit of land. If Sam was working anywhere near the road by Heathcote's place, Heathcote inevitably stopped and used the opportunity to set off on a rant about

Barnes and the fence he tore down, "without my say-so, mind! Don't you see, Sam?" he'd bellow, his red cheeks turning purple, and his meaty jowls quivering.

Sam would smile and offer the same answer every time: "Oh, I s'pose so."

That would make Heathcote bob his head emphatically, which inevitably dropped the long curl in his widow's peak right between his buggy eyes, which made his vexation look simply ridiculous.

"He tore down that cartway, Sam! Don't you see?"

"Oh, I s'pose so, Mr. Heathcote."

"He has no right, and he knows it!" This merited an index finger jabbing at the sky. "That cartway is perfectly legal and fair, don't you see?"

Sam knew that was a stretcher, but so what? "Oh, I s'pose so," he said.

One particularly chilly and windy May morning—perfect for keeping the new black fly hatch away—Heathcote and Barnes met on the road and got into it about the fence. This time Heathcote made good on his previous threats and slugged him good.

Heathcote was on foot, so he left Barnes on the side of the road and went to keep his planned rendezvous with some neighbors, who were then tasked with going to the aid of Barnes. Since Heathcote did not seem overmuch concerned, "I only used my fists," he said, they did not rush, and by the time they reached the location of the incident, Barnes and his wagon were gone.

John Meads: He's Still Alive!

At seventeen years old, John Meads looked like a teenager patched together with parts from a grown man. His hands were too big, his long ears sprouted tufts of hair, and his shoulders and forearms were brawny like a seasoned logger. John liked his town, he liked farming and liked most of his family's neighbors, too. He knew exactly why his Pa liked Heathcote in particular. Where else was Pa going to get cheap whisky on the sly? John didn't say nothin', but if Pa was buying from Heathcote, God knows how many more were doing the same thing.

That's what John was thinking about that morning when he hopped on his pony, set out to fill in the washouts and came upon Mr. Barnes lying by the side of the road, curled in an unnatural way, his head resting on a bloody clod of dirt. John reeled as he crumpled to the ground, turned the man over, and lifted his shoulders and head to his lap, praying to himself that Barnes would respond. Barnes' jacket was saturated with the blood that spurted from his mouth, and he hardly looked himself, with his head caved in a bit on one side and his face sagging under the weight of pain and shock.

But he was breathing.

John gently deposited Barnes back on the ground and stuttered words of encouragement, although he wasn't at all sure Barnes knew he was even there.

He stumbled getting up and flung his arm over his pony to ease the weakness in his legs for a second and catch a breath. What should he do? He had to get help. He glanced back at the man on the ground, then swung himself up on the pony so vigorously that he almost went right over the other side. He kicked the little horse into a dead run and headed straight for the spot that he knew Tom Carew was likely to be working nearby. Tom would know what to do.

Thomas Carew sworn: when I first saw Mr. Barnes after he was hurt he was standing up and fell as I came within two or three rods of him … I sat down beside him and he managed to get his head across my legs; I saw a lot of blood near where he lay. … I stayed with him until Mr. Knight came along with the horses; we put him in the wagon. I then thought he would not live five minutes; he throwed up blood from his mouth; I could not tell what had injured him. —Fergus Falls *Journal,* June 14, 1878

"Barnes was covered in blood. He'd get up, then fall down again. I asked him what was the matter, but he didn't answer.

24

I couldn't think what had happened, unless maybe his horses spooked, tossed him out, and his wagon run over him.

John Knight asked him where he wanted to go. 'Home, I guess,' he managed to get out. He spoke rational enough then, but he kept gettin' up and lyin' down all the way. When we come up on the swamp, John—Mr. Knight—asked him, 'Which way?' and Barnes says, 'To the left.' That was wrong, though, and made me think he was not in his right mind after all, because the horses got down in the mire and we had to unhitch the team to get 'em out. I stayed with him in the wagon, though, while John went for help. 'Drive on!' Barnes says, not knowing we wasn't even hitched up.

When John got back, we took Barnes home, dressed his wounds as best we could and sent for a doctor."

Marcia Peck, Will Barnes' Nurse

Doctor Crommett put Will Barnes in the care of Marcia Peck. She could be relied upon to follow his orders, but there was little to be done, if he was simply awaiting death. He might as well be looked after by the woman who kept his house and cared for his daughter, Lulu.

It was hard not to stare at her, though. Marcia Peck was extraordinarily tall. As she towered over many of the men in Deer Creek, were she not wearing a dress, she might have been mistaken for a man, at least from a distance. She had a soft look about her face, which was gentle, with sun-worn lines and two different colored eyes—one hazel and the other a yellow brown. She, however, seemed oblivious of her singular appearance, or just comfortable.

People opened up to her, and why not? She knew the intricacies of everyone's maladies from Deer Creek to Ottertail and all the way to Wadena, having nursed many of them, and had never betrayed a patient by passing along even a smidgeon of confidential information for tawdry gossip.

Now she would spend her time enclosed in a small room, likely awaiting the death of her patient and close friend since she was just a teen. Now, twenty years later, she would be alleviating his suffering with sips of bone broth and small draughts of laudanum. She suspected there was some truth to the claim that Will had attacked Heathcote first—he could be like that—but he didn't deserve to die like this.

She expected to be in the room when Will at last succumbed, and 18 days after the attack, the time arrived. She recognized the tug of the realm of the spirit, but it had never frightened her. It was transcendent … holy … and belonged to spirits, not to the living, she knew. She was but a privileged witness.

When Marcia Peck took the stand, having elicited from Mr. Barnes the complete story of his assault, she could just as well have been about to reveal long-lost Bible passages for the assembled audience. That Wednesday evening, she was thinking of Mr. Barnes … of Will … when she rose from her seat at the end of the front row bench. The full courtroom stopped whispering. A few glanced at her husband, Nathaniel Peck. He had barely moved since he first sat down.

Marcia knew Barnes two years before her marriage sixteen years earlier to Nathaniel, and she "resided in Barnes' house most of the time I have lived in Deer Creek," she testified. Sometimes her stepson, Freddie, lived there, too. All were "quite friendly," and on a first-name basis. She knew Barnes was divorced but did not know he took his child by force from the child's mother.

Then the woman who towered over the railing in the witness box, seemed transported to that slightly earlier time and place, and the entire assembly with her.

"'Now you may tell me,'" Mr. Barnes said to me. "It was out-of-the-blue, you see, so I didn't know what he meant," she told the Court.

"'All the news,' he told me. But Dr. Crommett had given strict orders that nothing be said to him about his case—nothing that would in the least excite him—so, I told him about the weather, the price of rye, that sort of thing. The next Friday morning, Mr. Barnes seemed much better, and he asked me what was ailing him. 'You have been sick,' I said. He then asked, 'What made me sick?' I told him that he had been hurt.

26

He asked me where and how, so I told him that we thought someone had struck him … over near the field."

Others' reports of the attack were well known by now, so those gathered in the courtroom knew what was coming.

"'I know it all now; I could not concentrate my ideas before,' Mr. Barnes said to me. Mr. Barnes, you see, was driving along when he met Mr. Heathcote, who had a club on his shoulder and some sort of satchel or pack on the end of it. He asked Barnes to stop, which he did, and asked if Barnes had pulled down the fence. Of course, he had, so Heathcote said, 'You had best not do it again!' But Barnes told him that he'd pull it down whenever he found it up. 'I will teach you,' said Heathcote, and dropping his pack, struck Barnes across the face with the club."

There were gasps from every corner of the room. "Club! He used a club!" was whispered among the audience. This easily constituted a weapon, and that warranted a murder conviction. The judge banged the gavel perfunctorily and waited until the crowd had fizzled out on the juicy tidbit.

"Jennie, one of Barnes' horses, started. 'You know she could never bear a stick raised near her,' Barnes told me. 'I tried to manage my team, but Heathcote clawed at my breast. Between the horses and Heathcote, I fell to the ground,' he said, clear as could be," Marcia testified.

With precision, the witness continued to relay bits of information until she was excused and made her way with impressive decorum to the end of the nearby bench. Her gentle expression never changed, and all ten fingers clutched a cloth purse that looked doll-sized in long fingers.

Marcia did not sleep the night the jury deliberated. That the jury did not decide that night, or even early the next morning, gave her some hope that Will would have justice. But Otter Tail County maintained its record of acquittals with a "not guilty" verdict at 11 a.m. the next day. Nathaniel brought her word and her tall frame disintegrated into a straight back chair by the window in Barnes' kitchen. She was fragments of herself, and the house was ghost-like around her. No Will. No

Lulu, who had been placed with an old friend of Will's, someone with a fine reputation and money.

Nathaniel sat with her and held her hand in silence. He could think of nothing useful to say and a few moments later, he left. There was no question now; she would leave Otter Tail County. Making the decision diverted her thoughts for a time and lifted the sadness burdening her enough to bear it.

Among the self-defense pleas, this verdict stands out, with its most elucidative evidence found in Marcia Peck's testimony. It should have put Heathcote away for years. Instead, Marcia herself may have been the tipping point that assured his acquittal.

Marcia had known Will Barnes twenty years previously when they both lived in another state, so Marcia's appearance in Deer Creek after Will Barnes settled there was no accident. One might logically presume that Nathaniel Peck knew Barnes, as well, since Marcia and Nathaniel had been married 16 years at the time of Barnes death. However, Marcia testified that she "lived with Barnes most of the time," and referred to Freddie, Nathaniel's son, born two years after her marriage to Nathaniel, as her "stepson."

Nevertheless, it was her husband Nathaniel who convinced the authorities to bring a second-degree murder charge, rather than manslaughter, against Heathcote, so one might presume that the three of them—Nathaniel, Marcia, and Will Barnes—were close. Their arrangement was convincing from a practical standpoint; Nathaniel and Marcia struggled to support each other, and Barnes needed to employ Marcia for childcare and housekeeping. But was there more to tell?

Marcia and Will may have been lovers, if Nathaniel and Marcia's marriage, at ages 19 and 18, had long since cooled—and Nathaniel didn't mind being a cover for their affair. This would explain Heathcote's "whoremonger" epithet thrown at Barnes during the attack. (There was plenty of cursing in testimony in all the crimes; nobody else used *that* word.) Barnes claimed to be divorced (which may or may not be true). He did, certainly, have a daughter named Lulu, who Barnes had "stolen away," according to the Court, from a woman presumed to be Lulu's mother. Marcia took care of Lulu for Barnes, and the little girl became quite attached to Marcia, who she called "Auntie." But Barnes' wish that Lulu stay with Marcia upon his death was not recognized by the Court, nor did the Court return Lulu to her mother. Instead, the little girl was whisked away and given to a Barnes family friend in St. Paul to raise.

So, why were both Marcia and Lulu's mother, never mind Nathaniel, not viewed as suitable? The answer lies in the social mores of the time. Marcia and Nathaniel were separated, and Barnes and his wife (if that's what she was) were divorced. In the Court's view, this spelled instability in a home, and, in fact, the Court was right in the end. Whatever Marcia and Nathaniel's commitment to each other was, it did not survive the murder of their friend, and not long after the trial Marcia moved to adjacent Wadena County, and in 1881 they divorced.

Nathaniel's obituary in the Deer Creek *Mirror*, June 16, 1910, said he married a "Mrs. Scott" [Carolyn Woodriff Scott] in Deer Creek in 1883. But as intwined as Marcia and Nathaniel's lives had been, living through Barnes murder in Deer Creek, and in a marriage that had lasted 19 years (at least on paper), Marcia did not even get a mention in the obituary.

Divorce or even separation was the sort of "dust" that would have been swept into a dark corner. Marcia may have earned some stature as a nurse, but if their estrangement as husband and wife was known (and in a tiny village like Deer Creek, it was), there was no way the Court could justify granting her custody of Lulu.

It's also conceivable that the sexual identity and/or preferences of one or more of this threesome did not conform to the mores in this time and place, and although they would not have been revealed in an official way, such information could have impacted the Court's decision.

But as financial circumstances often forced people to live with an employer and away from their own home, it was possible for the three—Marcia, Nathaniel and Will Barnes—to establish at least the appearance of an innocent arrangement, and it was more comfortable for the community to accept the ruse, if that's what it was. A strong "wind," however (such as a murder trial), and dust gets kicked up. Barnes death may have seemed almost providential to the people of Deer Creek: Marcia moved away, Freddie stayed with his father's family in the Deer Creek area, and little Lulu was given to a respectable and financially secure family far away from her father's ghost and his sordid end.

The prosecution was bucking two more influences. Heathcote's brother had hired Minnesota's most celebrated defense attorney, William "Bill" Erwin, to represent Heathcote. In the eight years since Erwin had moved to Minnesota, settling in St. Paul, its capital, the attorney had built quite a reputation. The ordinary folks of this newly settled outpost in Otter Tail County would have their brush with fame, and they were star struck.

This was the man who defended W.S. Heathcote, whose distinction was that he was a ready source for cheap—albeit illegal—liquor. Deer Creek and the rest of the eastern portion of the county could lose their hooch supply if Heathcote was locked up.

Heathcote had been at it so long that he must have had a large clientele, and he surely had learned to be discreet. Even so, in the end, another might come along to fill the need for liquor. But Bill Erwin's stature was irreplaceable.

A few years later the law finally caught up with Heathcote and his liquor trade. This minor infraction couldn't have provided much satisfaction for folks still situated on the Barnes side of the fence controversy; it was much too little and too late. Heathcote's attorney, Bill Erwin, continued to build his reputation in criminal defense work. He was, however, not above exploiting a situation with tricks of questionable legality. Evidence of this would come in a later case, and ultimately his shenanigans caught up with him. Heathcote's trial was the first time he had tried a case in Fergus Falls, but it was not to be the last, or even the most infamous, for Mr. William Erwin, Esq.

May 1884
INDICTMENT
The State of Minnesota against W.S. Heathcote

W.S. Heathcote is accused by the Grand Jury of the County of Otter Tail, in the State of Minnesota, by this indictment of the crime of selling spirituous liquors in a less quantity than five gallons without first having obtained a license therefore committed as follows: The said W.S. Heathcote on the 17th day of November A.D. 1883 at the town of Deer Creek in the county of Otter Tail in the State of Minnesota, did unlawfully sell spirituous liquor to Joshua Mead in a less quantity than five gallons to wit a pint without first having obtained a license therefore contrary to the forms of the statute and against the peace and dignity of the State of Minnesota.

5. A Famed Attorney Returns to Town, March 1882

DELIBERATE MURDER. HARVEY R. STULL SHOT IN COLD BLOOD FOR HIS MONEY IN TOWN OF COMPTON.

THE MURDERER, WM. CHRISTIE, ARRESTED AND IN JAIL IN THIS CITY.

HE CONFESSES HIS GUILT TO ESCAPE HANGING AND WANTS TO BE SENT TO PRISON FOR LIFE AT ONCE.

—Fergus Falls *Semi-Weekly Journal,* April 3, 1882.

The third unpunished murder is the only crime without a confirmed perpetrator, and the only acquittal not based on self-defense. It was reasonable to charge William Christie for the murder of his friend Harvey Stull, since he had both motive and opportunity; however, there was at least one other credible suspect. A man named Sherman had a motive; he was Mrs. Stull's lover. If a mysterious set of footprints at the crime scene was his, he had opportunity, too, and there was at least one person who had openly expressed his fear that Sherman was capable of murder. That was the victim, Harvey Stull.

Christie's help had been enlisted in a plan to whisk Stull's estranged wife away from the clutches of her lover, Sherman, in a daring rescue. This was never accomplished, in part because Mrs. Stull didn't want to be rescued. She makes only one brief appearance in this story; Sherman is glaringly absent.

Instead, William Christie was apprehended and terrorized by his captors' threats of hanging if he didn't confess, so he confessed. There were plenty of details, all circumstantial evidence, pointing squarely at Christie, but no one witnessed the shooting, so little more than a coerced confession was what the prosecution had. In today's legal system, this would not be admissible evidence, but such was not the case in 1882.

Capital punishment was part of Minnesota law since 1849 when it was not yet a state. "Death by hanging" was enacted into territorial law for cases involving premeditated murder. In such a case the judge was *required* to impose a death sentence. In 1868 the Minnesota legislature changed the law to provide for "death by hanging" only if recommended by a jury. Under this law, there were no hangings, as a guilty perpetrator could save his life by simply pleading guilty. This is the law referenced by Justice of the Peace Maltby when William Christie was in his custody after being detained, and what the terrified Christie saw as his lifeline.

The prosecution and the defense quickly turned to interviewing people with peripheral knowledge of events in the killing of Harvey Stull, and Fergus Falls *Journal* reported every smidgeon—relevant or not. Even the jury selection warranted a favorable mention.

... The jury are above the average in intelligence, and will enjoy the distinction of deciding one of the most remarkable cases that has ever been tried in this state. —Fergus Falls *Journal*, November 30, 1882.

But Christie seemed incapable of shooting anyone in cold blood, much less his good friend. His motive was so flimsy, and his execution of the crime and aftermath so sloppy that he was a very unconvincing perpetrator. Fortunately for Christie, his father had the funds to hire a good defense attorney and, hence, the county was buzzing once again with the return of Bill Erwin.

By this time, four years after Heathcote's acquittal, Erwin's fame was thoroughly vested throughout the state and beyond. There was little chance that a jury in Otter Tail County would be the ones to besmirch Erwin's reputation by handing him a loss. This brush with fame was one to be savored.

It didn't hurt that Christie was young and good looking, and he had a pretty wife and infant son, offering a scenario made in heaven for the super-charged litigator. Erwin must have felt untouchable in this milieu and pulled a trump card that he had no business having in his possession.

Isaac Roper and Horace Keith: It Wasn't a Wounded Deer, March 1882

There was still a good bit of icy snow leftover in the woods. Snowmelt during the day meant sloppy roads until after nightfall when the puddles in the wagon ruts would crust over as the temperature fell below freezing. That morning in late March, Isaac Roper and Horace Keith set out to haul ties for the railroad. They were a mismatched pair if there ever was one—Isaac tall and gangly, Horace short and stubby like a tree stump. They had followed the Deer Creek Road as far as it went before splitting off on the tie road towards a tamarack swamp. A little way in they saw some blood in the snow and figured it was a deer wounded, so they followed the trail, which was no trick, the two having hunted since they were old enough to hold a shotgun steady and not get knocked down by the kick.

"Low and behold, it wasn't no deer!" Horace reported. "There's a hand sticking out from under a brush pile! "Course we went for help, then, right away."

The pair found William M. Farr, who lived nearby and knew the area well. "We have found a dead man!" they announced, and all three returned to the brush pile by the tamarack swamp. This time, Farr saw boot tracks, but not just gum boots, which anybody with any sense would be wearing. A big track had settled in the snow and frozen.

"One a' them fancy leather Kip boots, looked to be. Now, I ask you, who'd be wearing Kip boots on a country road end a' March?" Farr mused.

"You fall on your arse, sure, never mind ruining the boots," Horace added.

Isaac Roper

Heard Christie got all the way into Douglas County before he was arrested in a blacksmith shop. If I was running from the law, I think I'd get my pony shod ahead of time, but maybe that's just me. I also heard that he says, "My God is Stull killed?" Now, if he killed him, he wouldn't need to ask, would he? Or maybe that's just me.

Meantime I helped to haul the body to the schoolhouse in Bluffton. We sent the kids home, but none 'a them went. Curious little buggers. It ain't right to keep a body in a schoolhouse, but that's what we done. The kids just tore around outside, mostly—it weren't that cold—until they felt good and ready to skedaddle on home.

Dr. Bedford didn't get there 'til a couple 'a days later, when he had us move the body to the back of Doty's place nearby. Doty's got a store in Bluffton and a few rooms to let.

Mr. Doty

First, they hauled Mr. Stull in and laid him out on a table in my back room. Maltby, who's Justice of the Peace in Bluffton, had issued a warrant for Mr. Christie's arrest. He and the coroner, Dr. Bedford, asked me for a room where they could hold Christie, too. Both had a hand on Christie, but it looked to me like he didn't have enough spunk to escape even if nobody was looking. When they brought him in to look at the body, Christie turned his face away. I could have sworn he got smaller right in front of me.

He asked me (me, of all people! I ain't the law!) "Will they hurt me?" I told him, "No, not as long as you are on my premises, and I can help it."

Then the oddest thing happened. This woman wrapped up in a fur cape, with one hand stuffed in a matching muff, waltzes in, says she's the dead man's wife, goes directly to the body, snatches up his hand and pulls a ring right off his finger. Then she turns to us with a look that'd melt a snowbank and says, "It's mine. I give it to him," and off she goes.

Well, she ain't been anywhere near Stull for a good bit, and the talk coming from New York Mills says she's been living in sin with a man name of Sherman. Maybe we shouldn't 'a let her done that, but Maltby didn't stop her. Wasn't my place.

Justice of the Peace Maltby

There had been some talk about what ought to be done with Christie, and some suggestions as to how peculiarly a certain tree in the schoolhouse yard was adapted to the purpose of a scaffold, but that don't amount to a threat in my book. I told him that if he confessed, he wouldn't hang, because that's the law, but if he claimed to be innocent, I couldn't say what might happen to him. I did say that, and it's absolutely true.

I asked him whatever could have induced him to do such a thing. He sat bent over and didn't look up, and in a voice so quiet I could not hear him without leaning in close, he said, "I killed him for his money." Now I know that the people around Compton and Bluffton have known this young man a long time and can attest to his character. So heinous a crime seems impossible, but they weren't there when he broke down and confessed, and I was.

Court Notes: *The case of Christie, indicted for murder, has occupied the court since Monday, Nov. 25. A jury was secured with some difficulty. … Christie, who is described as good-looking, with an intelligent face,* *sensitive, and calculated to create a good deal of sympathy, is attended by his wife and baby. Her mien and appearance are increasing the feelings favorable to Christie.* —Perham *Journal,* Late November–December 1882.

Wm. Christie, The Prisoner Sworn: *Prisoner said that after he was arrested at Spruce Hill, Dr. Smith told him how the body of Stull was found, and that the best thing he could do would be to plead guilty; that mob would hang him if he did not; that when they reached Bluffton there was 100 men in and around the store, where they showed him Stull's body, and where he heard men say in subdued tones; "He ought to be hung."* —Fergus Falls *Journal,* December 7, 1882.

The Defendant Takes the Stand

When the accused was called to testify on an early December day, it caused quite a sensation. He was just twenty-eight years old, and quite handsome, but the ordeal had marked him, plastering enduring dark circles under his deep, brown eyes. He'd cinched his belt at least a couple of notches tighter, gathering his trousers in small bunches of fabric that he no longer needed to cover his thinning frame.

His petite, blond wife pulled her lips together tight, raised up her chin and gave him a slight nod. With her modest, light-brown suit, buttoned over a high-collared, white blouse, her arms gently bouncing a sleeping infant, no defense attorney could have created a better scene for his client.

Will Christie, though, was terrified. It was never his way to get up in front of anybody—for any reason—even to do a report in school in front of his smirking pals. But this day there was no smirk, no giggling from the girls who couldn't resist his pretty-boy looks. This was beyond anything he could have imagined.

The courtroom strained to contain every adult who could afford to leave their tasks to watch the goings on of a trial that had mesmerized the county, and now the defendant himself would speak. It all but took their breath away.

As the young man settled himself with great care in the witness chair, as if he feared the chair would crumble beneath him, the shuffling feet stopped, coughs were stifled, and children were shushed with stern looks from any nearby adult.

He began. "I had been at Bluffton about a week before, when Stull, um ... Mr. Stull talked about going to New York Mills. See, he wanted to convince his wife to, uh ... come with him. ... to Iowa."

Then he stopped. It was mortifying to have to fight for his own life like this, in front of so many people he didn't know, but now he would also have to publicly acknowledge knowing all about the illicit relationship of his friend's wife—and admit to his role in Stull's plan to correct it. His face, pale with many months of incarceration, now flushed with the familiar panic of the schoolboy. Then he glanced at his wife, who wasn't looking at him just then. She was smiling at their baby, who he guessed was smiling back at her, and Will forgot—for just enough time—to be afraid. He had to speak up, speak clearly and do as Mr. Erwin, his lawyer, had instructed. He couldn't fail now! His wife looked up at him, still smiling, and he continued.

"Mr. Stull ... he wanted his wife to leave Sherman, a man he thought was dangerous, you understand. In fact, he even said that he might have to kill Sherman to get his wife back. That's why I asked, 'Is Stull killed!'"

The benches in the courtroom creaked in near unison and a rush of whispering voices flared and then came to a halt as Judge J.P. Williams banged his gavel and ordered, "Quiet!" Then he banged it again, just to make sure they got the message. Miraculously, Will's baby didn't even whimper.

"He wanted people to see us together on that road, but when they passed, we separated, but no one saw that. Yes, he gave me the trunk check for the train and the key. How else was he going to send it on to Iowa? That's why I had to mail that letter to his friend Graves with the trunk check and the key. Oh, it sounds so complicated now, but you have to believe this! He wanted his things sent to Wadena so that the people in

Bluffton wouldn't know he was going to New York Mills after his wife! This all had to be secret, or he had little chance, do you see? And that's ..."

Suddenly, Will dropped his head down and slumped. His wife was on her feet instantly, but Mr. Erwin's hand on her arm served as a gentle reminder to maintain decorum. Will was exhausted, and when he looked up, his eyes were swimming in tears. He straightened in his chair, tilted his chin down, pulled out a handkerchief and pressed it over his eyes for several seconds. Something between a deep sigh and a sob escaped from him, but it was just one. The courtroom froze in anticipation—even the children. The defendant raised his chin and looked straight ahead.

"I remember meeting George Northrup just after passing the forks in the road—him and another fellow. Stull wanted to walk with me until we'd passed those two. He wanted to be sure they saw both of us on that road. No, it's not the way most would go to New York Mills, but that was the whole idea, see? Stull was taking it so no one would suspect where he was going. And he walked slow, so it would be dark, too. He couldn't risk Sherman finding out, could he? After they passed by us, Stull took that cut-off road, and I never saw him alive again.

Will stopped but couldn't bear to look at his wife whose tears were dripping uncontrollably on the baby's blanket. Mr. Erwin rose to his feet, tugged at his shirt cuffs, tilted his head toward the jury and approached Christie.

"Just one question, Mr. Christie," the lawyer said with profound calm. "What did Mr. Bedford and Mr. Maltby say to you in that hotel room where you were first taken upon your arrest?"

"In, uh, B-B-Bluffton?" Will answered softly, stumbling over the words.

"Yes, in Bluffton. At Mr. Doty's?"

"They said ... there was no way under God's heaven for me to get out of this, and I better confess, or I'll hang!"

The packed house made no attempt to contain their reaction to this and erupted in raucous expressions of opinion. Mr.

Erwin told the judge, "No further questions, Your Honor," calmly crossed the floor in his polished leather shoes and stylish tailored suit with perfectly creased trousers and sat, eyeing the judge who banged his gavel fruitlessly.

The Arguments: ... *We come now to Saturday evening when everything conspired to call out a large audience. The interest in the case had been constantly increasing from the first, and now that it was raised about the city that W.W. Erwin would make his great plea for the life of Christie in the evening, the large hall of the courthouse was filled in advance of the evening hour, and still the throng kept pouring in. ... Such was the interest in the case and the wonderful eloquence of Erwin, that these people were content to stand there for three hours, while the truly great advocate wrestled as if for the life of a dear friend. ... Nothing was omitted in the wonderful three hours argument, and if any man who had heard it had any previous doubts that Bill Erwin is the greatest criminal lawyer in the Northwest, these doubts were then and there dispelled.* —Fergus Falls *Journal,* December 7, 1882.

"NOT GUILTY!"

THE VERDICT THAT DECLARES WM. CHRISTIE INNOCENT OF THE BLOOD OF HARVEY R. STULL.

GENERAL SURPRISE AT THE VERDICT.

ABLEST EFFORTS EVER MADE BEFORE A JURY IN THIS COUNTY.

THE GREAT MYSTERY OF THE BULLET—WAS IT THE SAME?

The Bullet: ... *One of the items of most consequence in aiding the jury to bring in an early verdict of acquittal was the discovery made in the jury room that the ball that killed Stull, although of the same caliber, was of a different mold from those left in the revolver and found upon the person of the prisoner. ... There is talk of the mysterious loss of this bullet in the court room during the trial, and of its recovering lying on the floor, and suggestion is made that it was not the one first put in evidence. But if* *cunning counsel could have exchanged this piece, they would scarcely have failed to have taken the opportunity to suggest the difference to the jury.* — Fergus Falls *Journal*, December 7, 1882

Justice Maltby and the comments of others about hanging, or even the danger of a lynching, didn't sit well with folks, including the "above average in intelligence" ones serving on the jury. Too many people milling around at Doty's store and hotel in Bluffton heard the comments, so "misinterpretation" was about the only excuse available to the prosecution.

When Stull enlisted Christie's help with the purpose of getting his wife back, it was a daring plan that one would not impart to any but a loyal friend. There may have been another who had unwittingly shared Stull's whereabouts with the real culprit—a man wearing fancy Kip boots, perhaps? Everyone, including Stull and Christie, were in rubber boots, so whose tracks were those?

When Bill Erwin produced the zinger in his closing argument that the bullet found didn't fit Christie's gun, the jury had the clincher they may have hoped for all along. As Henry Palmer, the jury foreman, told a Fergus Falls *Journal* reporter following the verdict, "I would have stayed there until maggots crawled out of the keyhole before I would have convicted that man."

Erwin's trickery might have done some legitimate good; his methods, however, were highly circumspect and still making the news forty-four years later.

THREE CHRISTIE JURORS LIVING

... In telling the story of the Christie-Stull trial, one of the reasons reported to have been given for the acquittal of Christie was that the bullet, which was submitted to the jurors, along with the revolver taken from

42

Christie did not fit the revolver. It is related that Mr. Erwin had possession of the bullet which was taken from the dead body of Mr. Stull, and while holding it up for the jury to see, he dropped it on the floor, apparently by accident. Someone sitting beside Erwin reached down and, so as far as the jurors could see, handed to him the bullet which he had dropped. But those who understand Mr. Erwin's methods and who were somewhat suspicious, maintained that the dropping of that bullet was prearranged and that the man who sat beside Erwin picked up a different bullet and handed it to him. ... It was these little artifices, which Mr. Erwin used most effectively in defeating justice and keeping men from the gallows who ought to have gone there. A trick of this kind, if detected at the present time, would undoubtedly result in disbarment, even of a man so widely known as Mr. Erwin. —Fergus Falls *Daily Journal*, July 20, 1926.

6. Taking the Law into Their Own Hands, June 1882

A writer in "The Century," noting the statement that in 1882 there were 1,266 murders in this country, of the perpetrators of which only 93 were legally executed and 118 lynched, remarks that "under any government where 1,173 murders out of 1,266 escape legal execution, it is a wonder that there are not 1,000 lynched instead of 11" How shall we suppress lynch-law? The writer answers this question in the only manner in which it can be properly answered, namely, by "increased care and zeal on the part of all citizens to secure the execution of the law." He adds, very truthfully, that if all men could rely upon the certainty of punishment following crime, there would be vastly less crime and no lynching. —The Democrat, sometime in 1882, referencing the popular magazine, The Century

For the Fergus Falls *Democrat* to use the high incidence of lynchings in the U.S. to support an argument for the death penalty is a stunning methodology, and it suggests that "getting away with murder" was not just a county issue but perceived to be a national problem. That it was called "lynch-law" is also telling, as if meting out justice without due process was another form of "law." Neither writer favored lynching, but their arguments indicate strong support for legal hangings as a deterrent to crime, a sentiment building as well for what was to come in Otter Tail County.

Around the time of the summer solstice in June, the late evening skies over the northern parts of Minnesota are draped in a filmy light that hangs on in dreamy colors from peach and amber, to soft blue and lavender. Unless low-hanging clouds obscure the endless sunsets, true darkness waits until closer to midnight. This was the time a group of ordinary citizens gathered in Perham and transformed into a mob. About 1:00 a.m. on June 14, 1882, the men stormed its jail, dragged out a 15-year-old boy, and headed for a telegraph pole on Perham's Main Street. They had a long, sturdy rope.

The crime he committed was without motive, save to elevate the boy's twisted psyche. Still, this doesn't explain the rage that broke into his jail cell. That anger was emboldened by the actions of a man named Rothpletz, Justice of the Peace in Perham and editor of the *Perham Journal*. Justice Rothpletz took the law into his own hands, too, when he side-stepped the plan to take the suspect directly to Fergus Falls; as the county seat, Fergus Falls had a more secure jail to incarcerate a prisoner, and it removed the suspect from the community still reeling from the murders committed among its own.

Instead, Rothpletz instructed Special Deputy Steve Butler to disembark with the prisoner (captured by Butler in the Dakotas) at Frazee City, where he loaded both in a waiting wagon. What he intended was unknown, even to Butler, who was just following orders. But Johnny Tribbets ended up in a far less secure jail in Perham. The Justice had now given the community that felt most wronged by Tribbets' senseless crime easy access to the boy.

Twelve years earlier, Steven Butler had just arrived in America from England, ready to take whatever work could be had. In his later years, he wrote the story of his emigration from England as a very young man. It's just one story of one immigrant, who, at the time, was as unremarkable as the rest. He couldn't have imagined the critical role he'd play in the county's law enforcement saga, including one of the darkest moments for the county—and for him. But it only happened once. Butler never again allowed a mob to make good on their threats, and he earned an honored place in the county's legal history.

Steven Butler: A Future Lawman Arrives, August 1872

By 1872, the British Isles were flooded with news about America—land, jobs and endless opportunity, if the ads from emigrant companies and the railroads could be believed. A seventeen-year-old boy, stuck in a place so small it couldn't rightly be called a village, believed it all, and in July of that year, Steven Butler saw tiny Cripplestyle in Dorset for the last time.

His oldest brother took him to Salisbury—a whole-day trip there and back for him—where Steven got the train to Liverpool. It was the first time Steven had seen a train. In fact, it was the first time he'd seen much beyond Verwood, a village an hour's walk from home, and here he was, crossing his native country for the first time just to leave it.

Steven had worked hard that winter and spring, saving every farthing and spending none of it until he had enough. It pained him to leave his big brother, who could not bring himself to get out of the wagon at the train station to say goodbye. The look on his face was one that would not leave Steven in his lifetime.

"Now, y' do something, boy!" he told Steven. "But y' do what's right."

An even larger and more boisterous crowd of emigrants was forming in Liverpool. Many, he learned, would be boarding the Hibernia with him the next day. When at last they hit the open seas, Steven did not so much as look back; he was too busy retching over the side. For eight days the ship tossed them about. Steven heaved most of the first three, but about halfway across, he found his "sea legs" and his stomach settled into the constant pitch and roll.

On the eighth day, he heard a lot of hollering and went on the deck. An excited group was yelling, "Land, land! It's America!" and others quickly poured toward the rails to get a look. Steven reached inside his pocket and felt the tickets safely tucked inside the jacket he had not removed since he put it on in Cripplestyle. They were going to take him all the way to the land of his dreams: Duluth, Minnesota!

It was easy to get swept up in the noise and activity of the big steamer maneuvering into port. For the passengers, the excitement was dampened by the rigors of the trip. They were exhausted, dirty and were now face-to-face with a place that bore no resemblance to where they came from. Steven's heart pounded behind that envelope tucked in his jacket. Little did he know, however, that he hadn't landed in America. This was a place called Quebec in Canada.

On land at last, he joined a queue facing a small window, because he recognized them as fellow passengers with him on the Hibernia and knew that some of them were going to America, too. The man at the window told him that he had three days on the train, and then six days by boat to reach Duluth. There were others going there; Minnesota was well advertised in England.

Exhausted from the sea voyage, Steven slept most of the train journey, interrupted only to eat a bit, and get off at stops to use a toilet. Emigrant travel was not so fancy as to have such facilities in the cars. But by now, they were acquainted and seasoned travelers on this last leg of their journey, sharing bits of news picked up on the docks, food bought from vendors vying for their business at many stops, and more stories from home.

It was a clear June morning when Steven made his way to the deck in time to see a deep orange and purple sunrise splashing against the schooner's sails and glinting like magic on the water. He was used to seeing land by now, since these were inland lakes that they'd been traversing, but the vessel was headed so purposefully toward a far shore that he felt certain he was at last within sight of his destination—Duluth!

There were plenty of men positioned on the piers, checking out the latest "cargo" regurgitated from the dozens of ships that appeared, sailed away and reappeared with new loads. They watched with narrowed eyes and tight lips, while quick, brawny men guided crates of unfathomable weight—and slid the trunks of the more prosperous passengers in perfect sequence to be claimed by their owners without them having to wait.

Steven spotted a man who had a sincere look about him who was hiring for the Northern Pacific Railway, and in a surprisingly short time, he had signed up. The man promptly sent him to a young village named Perham for a job on a work train. "A few hours and working already!" Steven thought, jubilant as he threw his bag up the step of the train near the docks and boarded. He inquired about the distance to Perham and was told, "not so far." His confidence soared as he left the jagged rocks that crawled out of Duluth harbor's dark waters and pointed to the sky, but he soon realized "not so far" was a relative measurement in this vast, new land.

Miles of spindly, pointed trees, huge, looming furry-looking ones, too. Wildflowers of every kind and color came crawling out of the woods and blossomed in profusion as they reached the sunny openings carved out by the laying of the track. "What a beautiful land!" he thought, and so impressed was he that he said it out loud. "This is a beautiful and wonderful land!"

At one turn, a great black bear and two cubs came lumbering out of the woods and were chased back in by the train's cloud of smoke and tremendous, loud clatter. Deer appeared often and, terrified, leaped back into the brush, their huge white tails straight up like flags. Foxes sometimes ran alongside, and birds swooped and called from treetop to treetop. It was a glorious journey! He stuck his head right out the window and let the hot wind pour over his face—a wind like he'd never known in England!

At last, he rested his head on the wall and fell in and out of sleep until the train's chugging and huffing took on a slower pace and came to a stop in a clearing within sight of a lake. The conductor came to the caboose where Steven had settled and said, "Get off. This is Perham."

"I wish to go to Perham," Steven answered. He wasn't quite awake and thought there might have been a mistake.

"This is Perham," the conductor said and tossed the young man's valise off the train.

But there was no Perham. There was a house. Its resident was the optimist who had named the place. The railroad was counting on there being a Perham soon, but Steven Butler was so new that it finally occurred to him: he would be among those creating a town named Perham. Or he could just stay with the railroad and help to build it on its westward trek until it stopped somewhere beyond the mountains. He heard it would eventually go all the way to the Pacific Ocean.

The wind had picked up and it made the maple leaves and white pine needles glitter under the evening sun. It was strange to have the wind pick up in the evening, but June was a volatile month for weather; he would soon learn that anything was possible in this month that was blossoming into summer. For the moment, he felt not the least bit of disappointment. The lake before him was shimmering. The doe and twin fawns that came out to drink at its edge delighted him and diminished the importance of his immediate predicament. He marveled at the profusion of daisies and tall, spikey, blue flowers. He wondered at the huge stands of mature trees—so different from those small groves that ringed the fields near Crippenstyle. And he thought of his brother's parting words, as he had every day since he'd left home. Steven took great stock in them: "Now, do something, boy! But y' do what's right, too."

The north eastern part of the county has been startled by the occurrence of another brutal murder, which occurred in the pine woods of Red Eye, where a boy of 15 years of age, son of a farmer of that place, and by name John Trevitt, murdered in cold blood a surveyor and his assistant, rifled them of their watches and money, bought a new suit of clothes with a part of the cash and struck for Montana to join the Cow-boys.

A DOUBLE MURDER, STEVE BUTLER ON HIS TRACK

Steve Butler well and favorably known here, and constable at Perham, is on the track of the young villain, and the latest is from Moorhead yesterday, where he had word that the boy had gone to Miles City, Montana, and thither Mr. Butler was rapidly making his way. —

Fergus Falls *Weekly Journal*, June 8, 1882. ["Tribbets" is spelled multiple ways in the news reports.]

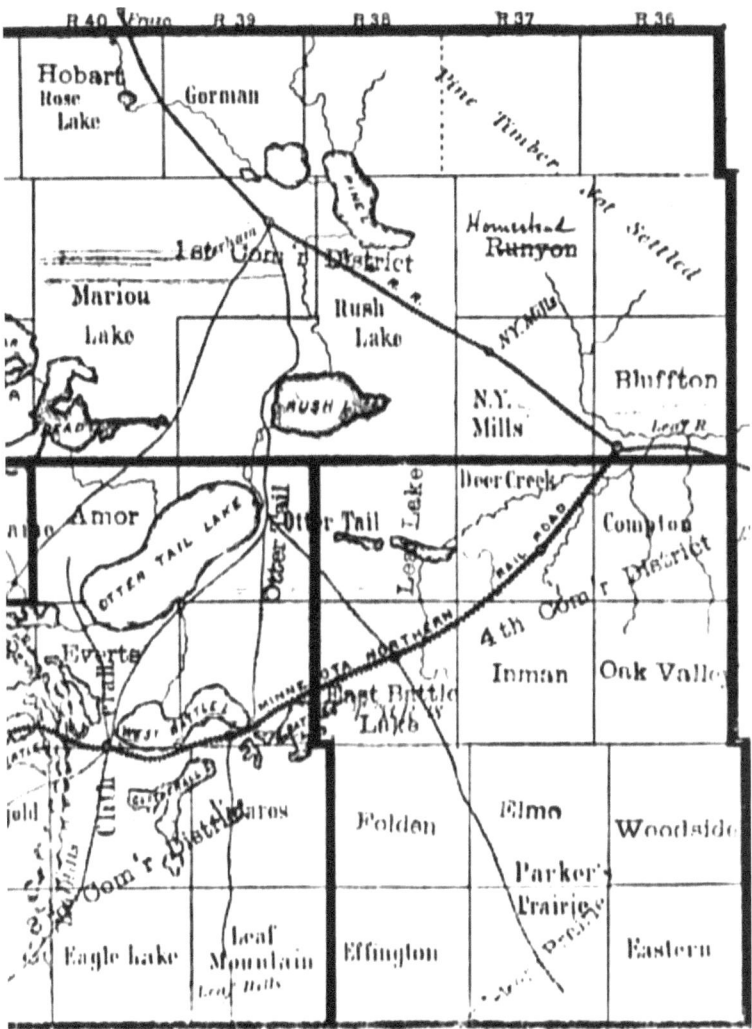

4. An 1884 map of Otter Tail County townships, cropped to show the "Red Eye", so named for a river that drops down into the northeast corner of the county. At the time, labeled simply "pine timber not settled," it was where the surveyors killed by Johnny Tribbets were working.

Cow-Boy, June 1882

Johnny Tribbets was a lanky fifteen-year-old. Soon the tufts of fuzz on his face would become a proper beard and his still-cracking tenor voice would be indistinguishable from a man's. Johnny was ready to become one of them ... Frank and Jesse James, Billy the Kid, the Youngers. Beyond these woods were open hills—even mountains! Full of canyons and draws where he'd hide out with his gang. He'd read the stories.

He knew he was meant to be an outlaw, but he would have to prove his worth. It was going to be so easy, with those two men staying right at his house. His younger brothers knew about him stealing the gun—and knew what he planned to do with it. His mother knew, too, but she was crazy, and nobody would pay attention to what she said. All the doctoring his father could afford didn't get anywhere with her, as far as young John could tell.

No, this was his time. Not that many people knew the surveyor and Fritz, so who would even think to look for them when they were missing? He knew they had money, so he could outfit himself pretty slick at Mr. Struett's store in Perham. Then off he'd go, all the way across the Dakotas where nobody would find him, unless he wanted to get found. By the time that happened, outlaw gangs would've heard about what he did, and those gangs would be fighting over who got to join him up.

That's the way it was going to be. He was going to be in a book one day, just like the ones stacked up under his bed, and everybody would be reading about his exploits. Sure beat slopping pigs and splitting fence rails, stuck on their sorry little farm, listening to his crazy mother and her crying about her "poor dead sister" and all. Someday he'd come back for his little brothers, and he'd head up his own gang. For now, he was headed to Montana and a whole new life.

TWO MEN FOUND DEAD IN THE PINE WOODS ON THE RED EYE, IN THIS COUNTY.

THE DEED OF A MERE BOY OF 15 YEARS, WHO HAD READ THE LIVES OF THE JAMES BOYS, AND WANTED TO BE AN OUTLAW.

—Fergus Falls *Weekly Journal*

August Mutschler: A Search Party

Red Eye. The last unsettled area of the county, heavily forested and named for a river that drops a loop down in the furthermost corner in the northeast of the county before heading back into neighboring Becker and Wadena counties. Perham, more than 20 miles to the west, is the closest village. A surveyor, Ed Washington, and a local boy, Leo Fernbacher, known as "Fritz" or "Fred," who Washington had hired to assist him, were headed deep into this near wilderness, boarding at the Tribbets' house and taking Sunday's meal at the Dornbush farm nearby. Sunday dinner was the last anyone saw of them.

Concern for the missing pair heightened when Johnny Tribbets showed up in town with a gold watch and a wad of money, outfitted himself in new duds and hopped the train heading west. A search party including T. C. Simpson, Peter Jung, C. Wetzel, August Mutschler and maybe a dozen more set out that same day to look for what had become of those surveyors. August didn't really know the surveyor, but he knew Fritz a bit, as Germans in the area stuck together. Simpson, being a surveyor, organized the search following section lines, thinking that would be the most logical place to find them. Simpson was correct.

They'd tramped through the woods near the Dornbush place for the rest of the day Thursday. It was thick with new shoots of buck brush, and equally thick with black flies and a fresh hatch of mosquitoes after a late-night shower. The search party was about to give up when a loud "caw!" cut through the brush snapping against their arms and their feet crushing twigs underfoot. August had heard plenty of crows, but something about this one made him stop. It cawed again, and he made his way to the area around the tree, from which the creature did not fly.

The lingering twilight of early summer did nothing to mask the awful truth. Fritz had been shot all right but escaped long enough for his killer to chase him down and finish him off with a blow to the back of the head with a hatchet then slice his throat from one side to the other.

August reeled in his fury at the sight—a countryman, and a young fellow, at that. "Nein!" he hollered. "Nein, nein, nein!" and the others came crashing through the brush to his side. None could remember being so angry, far worse than at a Farmer's Alliance meeting, and they could get plenty heated. This was a different kind of angry, more like a big oak log that burns hot all night. Those 12 searchers could just as well have been a jury for Johnny Tribbets; he was in far more danger than he knew.

It was too dark to keep looking for Mr. Washington, but he was quickly found in the morning, more mercifully felled with one shot to the back of the head.

You Won't See Me Hung by the Law, Mid-June 1882

Deputy Steve Butler had traveled 275 miles by train, stopping at every dive, variety theater and similar amusement, following a trail of sightings of the boy who relished flashing his fancy gold watch and planting one of his shiny Kip boots on a hitching rail where anyone who cared could admire this well-turned-out desperado. Butler was exhausted by the pursuit. At Bismarck, the last frontier town of any consequence for a long stretch, he had boarded the Blakely-Concord coach, which now waited for the ferry that would get them across the Missouri River.

Butler swung down and ambled to the other side of the stagecoach, giving the sturdy lead horse a scratch behind the ears. The horse dropped its head appreciatively, his two ears framing a picture of a skinny young cowboy nearby. It was young Tribbets, waiting to board the approaching steamboat, headed up-river. Butler drew his revolver and leveled it at the fugitive, ordering him to put his hands up. Tribbets played innocent.

Butler didn't move a hair. "Johnny, you know me and what I want of you," he said.

"Steve, I see it is no use," Tribbets answered. "I know what I have done, and I know what you want me for. Have they found the men? Will they hang me if you take me back?"

Letting his gaze jump to the river, where he could just make out the steamboat's smokestack behind the closest bend, the boy took a step backward, then another, watching the finger of the lawman, motionless on the trigger. "I guess I won't go," he said calmly.

Butler steadied the gun on the boy's chest. "The people of Perham sent me after you dead or alive, and it matters not to me which way I take you back. You must be the judge, but you're going back to Perham."

Unaware of the drama in progress, a young lady passenger rounded the back of the coach and seeing the cocked gun in Butler's hand, screamed and ran off—enough of a distraction for Butler to lunge for Johnny and click the cuffs in place on the kid's bony wrists.

Butler retraced his route, and delivered the prisoner precisely as ordered by Justice Rothpletz, disembarking from the train at Frazee, for some reason that Butler was not told. It was a long way—a good fifty miles—from Fergus Falls and its secure jail. That's where Butler thought he was headed. Frazee wasn't that close to Perham, either, for that matter, which was also a puzzlement. Then Rothpletz himself showed up driving a wagon.

Somehow, the residents of Perham got wind of the plan and the news built as quickly as a summer storm. Not only had Justice Rothpletz deliberately kept the news of Butler's progress from them, now they suspected he meant to cheat them out of the justice this crime against their neighbors and their community demanded. What was going on?

In short order a gathering mob had got up the money to hire teams to intercept the prisoner, with others on horseback covering every route to the county seat. The roads were soon a cloud of dust, and anybody on the flats above Otter Tail Lake could have marked their progress as the clouds rose above the tree lines. There! There was the wagon! Rothpletz was leaning over the reins, the team at a full gallop, straining to outrun the mob closing in, with their shouts of "Rope! Rope! Hang him! Hang him!"

Rothpletz ran the team full bore right up to Col. Shea's new hostelry in Perham, where Special Deputy Butler burst through the door and bounded up the stairs with his prisoner.

There Butler shoved his man into a room, leaving the door open and facing the people, who in a great crowd rushed up after him, said: "Friends, there he is, you can look at him, but the one that hurts him until he has had a hearing will have to hurt me first." The crowd cheered the brave little man who at the risk of his life had followed his man 275 miles and brought him back to the scene of his horrible murder. The crowd after cheering him said: "He shall have a fair hearing and we won't touch him until he has had it."—Fergus Falls Weekly Journal, *June 15, 1882*

So, they had their culprit back home where he belonged, and Rothpletz—whatever that snake was trying to pull off—be damned. The hearing was assembled on the spot and by late afternoon, it was completed, and the brother of the dead surveyor faced the murderer.

"Well, I did kill your brother. I suppose you would like to cut my throat. But shake hands." [said Tribbets]. Washington recoiled. "Young man," said he, "I will not hurt a hair of your head, and may God forgive you. I can't. But I will not rest till I see you dead." The young villain promptly replied: "You won't see me hung by the law."

—Fergus Falls Weekly Journal, *June 15, 1882.*

A troubled kid, Butler thought. Little connection to the realities of what he was facing. You'd think he'd show remorse—or no emotion—but the boy seemed to enjoy the attention during his examination ... "laughing and grinning half the time, and he freely shared details about the murders with apparent pride," is the way the *Journal* put it.

Washington was sitting by a marsh looking at his plat, "and I just thought," said the boy, "of pictures I had seen in novels of men being killed in that position, and I drew my shotgun from my shoulder, just like that," suiting the action to his words, *"and I shot him through the back of the head. He never got up. Fritz, who was a little ways off, then came at me with his hatchet ..."*—Fergus Falls *Weekly Journal*, June 15, 1882.

Johnny was indeed relishing the small but rapt audience he had in describing the crime ... how he rolled the dead surveyor over and found a revolver, as one would expect with someone who spent long days in remote and wild environments. He fired at Fritz, but the young assistant turned and ran. Fritz was fast, but Johnny was young, too, and took after him. In the scramble to escape, Fritz fell, and Johnny drew his knife, but it broke in his hand.

So many opportunities for his life to be spared! Butler felt sickened. As if the scene couldn't get more gruesome, Tribbets finished the boy off with a hatchet. But the crime took one last bizarre twist. Butler pulled out his handkerchief and coughed. An excuse to also dab at his eyes.

"He asked for water, and I went to the creek for water and had nothing but my hat to bring it in. When I got back he was dead."—Fergus Falls *Weekly Journal*, June 15, 1882.

The mob kept their promise to wait until after the hearing, but not for long. It was one o'clock in the morning when the anger boiled up again. The flimsy Perham jail outer door was no match for the crowd of angry men.

"… The lynchers found hard work breaking in the door of Tribbet's cell. The sounds of the blows upon it could be heard a great distance. The crowd kept coming closer and closer but were warned back in menacing tones by the lynchers. At last the door yielded to their blows, and their victim was at their mercy. They took hold of him roughly, and he exclaimed, "Don't, boys; this is too rough." "G-d d-d you, you will think it rough!" was the harsh answer."—Fergus Falls *Weekly Journal*, June 15, 1882.

Butler learned that there were folks who tried to follow. Some were just curious; others may have hoped to prevent compounding the tragedy. But pistols glinting under the moonlight convinced them that following for any reason would be a dangerous business, and they certainly weren't going to tell the deputy just who those men were with bandanas tightly wrapped around their faces.

August Mutschler: A Lynching

"The boy thought he was going to get off!" said one. "He didn't feel the least bit bad."

"No sir! Not a whit!" said another.

"Damn proud of it, he was!"

"If Butler had not gone after him and got so lucky to find him by Bismarck, this *gör* would be joined up with outlaws," August Mutschler said, stabbing his finger in the direction of the boy who stumbled in front of the mob, a rope draped around his neck.

"God knows how many he would kill before getting strung up like that out West, but strung up just the same," an old farmer chimed in, and August gave him a nod.

A ladder was braced up against the telegraph pole and a rope thrown over one of the rounds. The men fell silent as the gravity of their actions hit home. All but August, who lit a match, stuck it under the boy's nose, and growled, "Smell that, you bastard. You'll be there soon!" and the rope end, flung over the pole, wriggled to their waiting hands.

The moon slipped behind a huge, dark cloud. The men shifted their feet and finally commented to each other. Low voices. Short, gruff phrases. By one-thirty in the morning the boy's legs stopped jerking and he swung ... gently ... for just a few more minutes. The *schlauer junge* was silenced for good.

August marched straight home. All the talk was about this poor family—boys, mostly, all running loose like feral cats. His *mutti* was crazy. Everybody knew this. August's wife was standing outside the back door.

"Goddamn that boy!" the man hissed. "*Verdammt!* I would not do anything so lawless, not in my life! But if you're going to, pick somebody worthless like that Tribbets kid.

It ain't right, you know," his wife said softly. "*Nicht richtig.*"

"Son-of-a-bitch."

She left her husband to fume in the patch of yard between the house and the outhouse and went inside to heat a cup of milk.

Coronor Bedford received the following laconic dispatch from Perham, signed Steve Butler: "Another man found dead—hung to a telegraph pole." The coroner proceeded to Perham, and an inquest resulted in the following verdict: "Died from strangulation at the hands of parties unknown." —Fergus Falls *Weekly Journal*, June 15, 1882.

> For altering legal protocol and refusing to bring the killer to the county seat in Fergus Falls, Rothpletz was dubbed "the Mephistopheles of the [Perham] *Journal*," and labeled "Judge Lynch" by the Fergus Falls *Weekly Journal*, as if he alone were to blame for what transpired. A year later, Rothpletz folded the Perham *Journal* and moved away. Still, if Tribbets had shown any kind of remorse, or even respect for the

legal process, he might have been allowed a proper trial.

The lynchers were never prosecuted, although many, if not all (in addition to Mutschler) were known. Special Deputy Steve Butler, hailed as a hero for his extraordinary effort in capturing the boy, surely felt a deep disappointment that the law, faced with more powerful social forces, could not prevail. He had reason to be fearful, too; threats of mob violence did not end with the boy's death, or even with this case.

7. The Homicide That Wasn't, January 8, 1884

"Effington Homicide!" the Alexandria newspaper proclaimed. Understandable, as every indication was that the victim would die by the time the issue hit the streets. Except that he didn't.

Had it been a homicide in Otter Tail County, it may very well have added to the "unpunished" list. But county lines had some significance. Effington Township occupied the extreme southern edge of Otter Tail, where a moderately believable self-defense avowal would do (or a defendant who was for any reason more likeable than the victim). But because the presumed homicide took place in Alexandria, which is in Douglas County, Otter Tail's more lenient interpretation of the law was not going to help John Arkan, who nearly killed his friend and neighbor, Ludvig Krueger.

How Krueger survived not just the attack, but the treatment afterward is not explained. A descendant of Ludvig Krueger said the family had never heard of the story, but that's not surprising. A family would be inclined to let an incident like this melt into the past and stay there.

The following is a report of the affair as it was given to us: Ludvig Kreuger and John Arken, farmers from the town "of Effington, Otter Tail County, were in Alexandria, Tuesday, getting some grain ground. By eight o'clock in the evening both men were slightly intoxicated and ready to start home. —Perham *Bulletin,* January 17, 1884. [iii]

Mr. Hensel, Alexandria, Minnesota, January 1884

"Here come these two hayseeds from a place called Effington right across the border into Otter Tail County, looking like they ain't seen a saloon in how long. My place, Hensel's Saloon, you know, must've looked mighty attractive, 'cause by about 8:00 o'clock they were both good and full. Kreuger, one said his name was, and the other guy was named Arken. Kreuger was small and wiry with a big nose and close-set eyes, a little like a troll, I thought. Arken was more like a barrel with legs. Walked kind of like that, too. Quite a pair! Just made you smile lookin' at 'em.

I had just brought out a new keg and went in the back to lock up. When I got back, the bar was pretty stacked up with men wanting their whisky and that got me distracted for a bit. I didn't notice that missing keg until I heard men outside hollering about a fracas of some kind. Arken had made off with it! Then he puts the keg in Kreuger's sled! If they was just having a little joke, I guess I could've had a good laugh, too, but Kreuger was steamed, said he didn't want to be taken for a thief and goes and puts it in Arken's sled!

That got them to arguing and fussing when Arken grabs a sled pin and cracks Kreuger over the head with it. He must've hit him just right, because that man dropped like an anvil and didn't move. Folks watching all this picked up Kreuger quick enough, paying no attention to this Arken fella, and hauled Kreuger off to Dr. Ballentine's right close by here."

Dr. James Ballentine, Alexandria, Minnesota

"The man was insensible—and quite drunk—when a he was brought to me, just as I had finished my supper. I live near Hensel's saloon where the incident occurred, so it was understandable that I would be tasked with helping the poor man. I saw right away, however, that I must call for Dr. Ward, who brought Dr. Vivian and Dr. McEwan. They found a crack five inches long across his skull, which was troublesome enough, but when they removed a one-inch piece of his skull and discovered a broken artery they felt there was no possibility he could live through it. The man's wife was sent for."

... Arken remained in town until 10 o'clock Wednesday but was not arrested. During the morning he called on Dr. Ballentine, and learning that his victim would probably die, skipped for parts unknown. — Perham *Bulletin,* January 17, 1884.

John Arken

Parts unknown? I went home! Where else would I go? John dropped the Alexandria *Post* on the floor and stared at the cup of coffee—now cold—on the table. There was one bite out of the slice of bread and a mouse-like nibble missing from the wurst—a still life on a plate next to the cup.

What was he supposed to do? Surely the Douglas County Sheriff could find him if he wanted to! Would Otter Tail County do anything? That didn't seem likely. So, he went home. Of course he went home! He put on his coat and hat, grabbed the canvas wood carrier and headed out to the wood pile. The frigid air knocked him out of his nervous exhaustion for a few minutes, but he dared not let Mary out of his sight for long.

He was terrified that she'd leave him over this. At any moment, she'd pull off her apron, throw it on the floor and disappear into their tiny back bedroom. She'd take the clock from Würrtemberg that was a wedding present, her Sunday dress and all the egg money. He pictured her doing this, but not because she had threatened to. She said almost nothing to him.

He stomped the snow from his feet and dropped an armload of wood in the bin.

"The newspaper said 'homicide'," she said.

"But Mary, Ludvig ain't dead! He'll pull through! He's young yet, you know," John replied, as calmly as he could. It was such a relief to hear her speak of it!

Mary stabbed at the fire in the cook stove and slammed the door.

Ludvig Kreuger, the Effington farmer whose injuries we reported last week is still living. He suffers but little pain and is conscious most of the time, but is gradually growing weaker, and it is thought his death is only a matter of time. —Alexandria *Post,* January 18 or 25, 1884.

"Ol' Ludvig could just fool them all," he added. It was one thought that comforted John. "You better go see for yourself," she said with a sigh.

She was right. That could mean jail. This was Douglas County, not Otter Tail. Jail. John Arken arrested and in jail. He tore off a piece of the bread and forced himself to eat it. It wouldn't do to be weak. Not now.

Mary took a *honigkuchen* out and dropped it with a clatter on top of the cook stove. Now the cake would fall, and she would curse loudly. The girls were at school, and she didn't care what her husband thought of her course language.

What would become of his girls? Luzie at 17 was old enough to have a serious beau and marry, but who would have her now? Her younger sisters would get teased mercilessly in school. Would they ever forgive him? And what of Mary? If she stayed, could she keep the farm up? He'd never even imagined such a thing before.

… Last Saturday the man Arken, who, as he expresses it, "smashed" Kreuger, returned to town and was locked up. Monday he had a preliminary examination before Justice Hutchinson and was remanded to jail to await the effects of said "smashing." —Alexandria *Post,* January 18 or 25, 1884.

District Court—Last Wednesday morning the jury brought in a verdict, in the case of State Vs. Arken, of guilty as charged in the indictment, and Arken was sentenced to three years in the penitentiary.
—Douglas County *News,* May 8, 1884.

Luzie Arken

She had always looked after her sisters, but not necessarily with this level of intent. The younger girls were now prone to fits of tears that rendered them as incorrigible as toddlers. "You're not my mother!" Anna would scream. Amelie would start wailing and retreat to the barn to tell her troubles to the newborn calves.

Margaretha would have none of it, but at 15, she was already capable of running a house on her own if it came to that. It sometimes did when Mutti and Luzie were in the barn, or in town for supplies. Anna was the baby—still eight years-old—and did nothing for herself that she could get her older sisters to take on.

It wasn't always like this—or at least not in this heightened state. It was hard to have Papa gone, but it was far worse to never speak of him. Luzie tried. Mutti flung the wooden spoon dripping with *schwarzsauer* across the room and whirled to face her daughter.

"*Nein, nicht mehr,*" she said, and that was that.

Luzie was industrious enough to get her hands on the newspapers, though, and learn what happened after Papa went to court in April. He told the judge that he was not guilty, but she didn't understand how that could be.

Mr. Kreuger thankfully had lived through it, but his head never looked quite right, she thought. He was getting out a bit by then. She saw him in church once and looked away. She didn't go to church any more after that, but she made her younger sisters go. They could ride the horses double and not have to hitch the wagon. Mother always stayed home on Sundays. It was the one day she allowed herself a rest—from all of it.

Luzi had heard talk that Otter Tail County never would have put Papa away like that. "Don't even lock up a murderer," a neighbor, Mr. Haugen, had said, and then he had a good laugh over it. She didn't think it was funny, even though she supposed he was trying to offer her some comfort. Papa was locked up and that was that. She would be working like a farmhand, not a lady of the house.

8. A Lyncher Dies a Violent Death, January 1884

Public opinion is decidedly against the practice of "thumpers" wrecking personal vengeance upon inoffensive citizens of inferior strength. Our Perham correspondent [a reporter for the Democrat] condemns the carrying of concealed weapons, and in the main he is right. But what is a decent man to do when he is attacked by a saloon bully or plug ugly and can but get away from him? Take a thrashing, be knocked down, disfigured for life, or perhaps kicked or beaten to death? ... A man who attacks another and is told that he will be killed if he does not desist, certainly takes his life in his own hand and is alone to blame if he loses it. —The Telegram, January 1884, *quoted in* The Democrat, January 31, 1884.

Perham saloon owner August Mutschler was one of the searchers who helped to find Johnny Tribbets' victims—and a confirmed participant in the mob who lynched the boy. This, however, had nothing to do with Mutschler's own violent end.

Mutschler and his wife could just manage to feed their eight children keeping a saloon on Perham's Main Street, but if the Village Council followed through with plans to raise their liquor tax, Mutschler's thin margin that kept his family going could be wiped out. He lost his temper, as he sometimes did, and threatened to burn the whole town to the ground. Nobody believed him, except John Sterner, who thought it was his responsibility to tattle. The Council investigated and let the matter go, but Mutschler would not. Sterner was now the target of a man with a temper who had the physical wherewithal to make good on a threat; Sterner, who was no match for the man he angered, took to carrying a revolver for protection.

It's not much of a stretch to deduce where this could go, which it did, and as quickly as a shooting was reported, the three Fergus Falls newspapers took sides, and the swiping began. (As Sterner was the brother-in-law of a Perham newspaper publisher, this could have been a trigger.) *The Telegram* launched an incendiary statement in support of Sterner; the *Democrat* polarized the squabbling with its daring call for gun control.

Sterner, who was in violation of the law of the land when approached by Mutschler, in carrying a concealed weapon, is in custody of the law to await the verdict of his peers, summoned under the forms of the law. What that finding is to be, no one can tell, but if it should be acquittal his whole future will be blackened and miserable by the ever present thought that in one brief moment of time, impelled thereto by the devil, and with the devil's deadly weapon on his person, in violation of law, took the life of a fellow mortal, and deprived a wife and eight children of husband, father and protector. The Democrat most earnestly urges the authorities to enforce the law against carrying concealed weapons. Nine out of ten murders, as in this case, are due solely to the fact that one or both parties have this devil's invention, the pistol, on their person. Had Sterner been unarmed at the time of this meeting, he might have got a black eye and a few bruises, but Mutschler would have been alive and he [Sterner] would not now be in a cell charged with murder. Banish the revolver. —The Democrat, January 31, 1884.

Had the state's concealed-carry law been supported in practice as well as in theory, the argument about who was the guilty party—the dead man or his killer—would have been moot. The law was interpreted to accommodate personal interests—and perhaps to squelch cultural differences, as well. Then, in a surprising twist, *The Telegram* paused in its attack of the *Democrat* and expressed a similar view about handguns, albeit from a different angle: *"The whole affair is another illustration of the evil results attending the habit of young men carrying revolvers—a thing that in a peaceable town like Perham only a fool, a knave or a coward will do."* But the sparring continued. *The Democrat* accused the *"maggoty little Telegram"* of *"very unjust and intemperate comments."* *The Telegram* condemned *The Democrat* for *"attempts to provoke prejudice against a brother publisher who has become somewhat involved in the case because the man who did the killing happens to be a brother of his wife."*

The Fergus Falls Journal, a Republican newspaper editorially, jumped onboard, claiming "The animus of The Democrat is quite discernible: the desire to injure Love, a rival Democratic publisher, and to generally solidify itself with Mutschler's friends."

E.H. Love was stuck in the middle. The editor and publisher of the new Perham *Bulletin* had inherited a distrust of the media provoked by Rothpletz and his now-defunct Perham *Journal.* But he was also married to the perpetrator's sister. To his credit, he took the high road and penned a graceful statement that was published in all three Fergus Falls papers.

"Never before has it been our lot to chronicle an event which has so saddened the lives of many and taken from the world a husband and father without a moment's notice. The sad tragedy of Saturday evening last in the shooting and instant killing of Mr. August Mutschler, of this place, by J.C. Sterner, is a deplorable affair, and can but arouse the deepest feeling of sympathy for the widow and fatherless little ones. We think not of ourselves, or the parents, brothers and sisters of the man who committed the crime. Although he is as an own brother to us, we uphold no man, were it our father, who would commit such a deed, and we want to see the law take its course. …" —Edward H. Love, editor and publisher of the *Perham Bulletin.*

It was wise of Mr. Love to tread lightly. As quickly as Sterner turned himself over to Deputy Butler, who took the prisoner to the hardware store Butler owned, a *"wild mob showed up,"* the *Fergus Falls Journal* reported, and *"demanded that Sterner be placed in the village jail."* Butler couldn't allow another disaster like Tribbets' lynching. So, flanked by supporters Doc Lindlay and Sam Wallace, who had tagged along with the mob of mostly Germans like Mutschler, Butler not only refused, but he also *"threatened to shoot any man who touched foot to the threshold."* The mob *"slunk off to get another drink, lay plans and look for reinforcements,"* as the Fergus Falls *Journal* characterized it.

It was late at night by this time. Butler immediately set out on foot with his prisoner. The sub-zero temperatures common in January had tempered a bit. The snow crunched under their boots but had lost the distinctive squeak of colder weather. With no wind, the exertion of walking kept them warm ... that, and the prospect of facing a larger—and more intoxicated—mob.

Lindlay and Wallace had a team sent out to intercept the lawman and his prisoner at Marion Lake about eight miles away. After an early breakfast at the Burgess farm in Amor Township, a bit farther on their route, they hurried the last forty miles by wagon to Fergus Falls, where Sterner was safely locked up in the county jail.

But it still wasn't over. The Telegram reported, "The Germans are very much incensed at E. H. Love ... and are threatening to drive him from the town ... indignation meeting will be held tonight."

Butler, now back in Perham, asked the sheriff in Fergus Falls to appoint another deputy, but was told this could not be done by telegraph. Instead, Deputy Butler was reminded that *"every man is a conservator of the peace,"* and he should call upon the citizens as needed. That worked for a while, but if Sterner was acquitted, Butler would need more muscle if he had any hope of keeping the peace, never mind saving his own skin.

Perham's robust lumbering trade gave him the solution: lumberjacks. Given that they were accustomed to facing danger every day, and they were, of necessity, physically powerful, lumberjacks were exactly the kind of "conservators of the peace" required.

Research into Mutschler's case yielded extant court documents with testimony from a long list of witnesses. One of the most intriguing stories, though, was not found in the court documents. It was recorded in brief in *The Democrat* and nowhere else.

The reporter did not bother to give the person testifying at the coroner's examination a name. He has been named "Old Jim" in this account, a person derisively dismissed, but as an eyewitness, he may very well have known much more than given credit for. Perham's saloons were important gathering places and yielded many witnesses who provided testimony in this crime. But none of them were positioned as well as "Old Jim" to pick up on key details.

The Comfort of Mutschler's Saloon

August Mutschler was a feisty, short, blocky German with bulbous forearms blanketed in dark hair. "Nein!" he'd bellow and hold up his fists in the apparent direction of the Perham Village Council. "Nein! This town will amount to nothing if they raise the fee for their goddamn license! They want to drive me out of business! Nein! Yah, I said I would burn the town down! Goddam that son of a bitch John Sterner! I'm going to whip that son of a bitch! What does he mean running to the council like a schoolboy, tattling!"

"Hallo, August," Christian Huntsinger said, plopping down next to Joseph Palmer.

"Palmer, I tell you! He's trying to ruin my reputation in this two-horse town!

"Mutschler! Stop your ranting and get me a beer," Palmer hollered over the noise of pails banging around behind the bar. One got in Mutschler's way and was sent crashing against the front door with a powerful kick. The stocky man paused long enough to slam a heavy mug of his home-made beer in front of his customer, the foam sloshing over the edge and running in slow rivulets down the bar. Palmer rescued the dice box before it, too, was bathed in it.

"That son of a bitch!" the man behind the bar roared, slamming a beer in front of Huntsinger, too. Huntsinger was new in town, but Palmer was a regular, who showed up most days soon after the shade went up in the big front window.

Some of Mutschler's customers ate there every day, having no means to cook a meal where they roomed, and preferring the relaxed camaraderie of the saloon to the façade, at least, of propriety typical of a rooming house. August kept long hours, and he worked hard.

His customers took note. "How'd he ever find the time to have so many kids?" they'd joke. Everybody would have a good laugh and August would lap it up.

"I'm up to eight!" he'd say. "I'd have twice that many kinder if she could just keep up," he'd roar, and the laughter rose to the rafters and bounced among the boots stomping the floor.

The stomping also kept their feet warm. The big wood stove had the room comfortable enough to shed their heavy woolen jackets, but the floor never warmed up much in the winter.

"Let me tell you something, you boys," he said, finally in a calmer tone of voice. "If you see that Sterner son of a bitch so much as set foot in the street in front of this saloon, you better see to it that I know before anybody else does. There's a beer on the house for that, too," he said in a low rumble, the saliva on his big lower lip quivering right in their faces.

Mutschler loved his saloon. Truth is, his customers felt safe there, and for all his bombast, he was as straightforward and honest as any man on Perham's Main Street. Some saloon owners had bouncers, but not Mutschler. He'd hold up his fists in front of anybody who'd suggest such a thing and say, "These here are my bouncers, see?"

All the shouting and clatter gave the laborers a kind of entertainment that suited their own rough ways. If they were lucky, eventually they'd get hired by the lumber companies, which meant regular wages all winter. It was damn hard work, and it took tough men to survive the dangers in the woods— and the drinking at the end of the week. Loggers loved to drink and dance, destroying the surface of a wood floor with their caulked boots; the spiked-soled boots were often the only footwear they owned. They loved to fight, too, but it was only fists for that crowd—no knives or guns.

In the meantime, other men would wait. Soon enough they'd be hauling ties for the expanding railroad and lumber for the constant building to catch up with the stream of settlers that chased the railroad's path west, or they'd be sent to repair roads rutted with the spring's thawing and freezing. But in January the pace of life slowed like tree sap and allowed friendships to rekindle over the smell of beer, wood smoke and wet wool.

Mutschler had his regulars, or new folks in town who made their way from one establishment to the next, breaking through the confines of a Minnesota winter, hemmed in by deep snow and limited daylight. Another bar, another wood stove, another card or dice game wasn't exactly variety, but it would do. They knew Mutschler had alienated plenty of people, and they didn't have to stay there. But mostly they stayed.

"That prissy John Sterner," one said. "Running off to the village council like a momma's boy! He's got no business …" More grumbles in agreement.

Missed Opportunity

Old Jim wasn't actually that old, but an undiagnosed health condition had gradually added to the hump on his back and rheumatism bowed him further and slowed his movements. Long ago he had abandoned the tonics recommended to him—every one of them having side effects as bothersome as the constant dull pain—and chose instead the comfort of one of the bars on Perham's Main Street.

If he was lucky, Mutschler or Rush's kid—or whoever was tending bar in whatever bar Jim was in that night—would set a mug down in front of him with a nod and that would be that. If he wasn't so lucky, some ass-wipe would holler out, "J-J-Jim would l-l-like a puh-puh-punch," and a few of the joker's friends would snicker and turn their backs on him. Jim wasn't just strange to look at; he had a stammer that could challenge the most patient listener, so he'd learned long ago that his best shot at making his way in the world was to keep his mouth shut.

Since listening to Jim talk was more taxing than most people cared to endure, they just ignored him. In time it was suggested that his hearing was bad, too, and he'd heard the word "idiot" tossed around as well. Neither of those was true, but it meant that Jim overheard a lot—the usual gossip and drivel traded among the bars' regulars, and since he never reacted to what he heard, (who was he going to tell?) the participants in these conversations barely noticed that he was there.

He got pretty good at lip reading, too.

The night August Mutschler came into Rush's Saloon, Old Jim was at the bar. Somebody told the coroner, and Jim, along with a raft of other witnesses, was sworn in at the inquest.

... A ridiculous phase creeps into almost every human event. The Perham tragedy proved no exception. Among the witnesses examined by the coroner was one of those knowing characters always around on such occasions. This one had an impediment in his speech. Having been sworn he was asked by the coroner to tell what he knew of the affray, and commenced: "W-well, I was s-standing at the b-bar in Rusch's s-saloon w-when a man came in and g-going u-up to another s-said you are a l-liar and I can li-lick you."

"Well?"

"T-then the other man b-backed away a l-little and p-pulled a revolver."
"What then?"
"W-why I j-jumped behind the bar."
"Is that all?"
"N-no! S-somebody s-shot and I j-jumped behind the ice box."
The witness was excused. —The Democrat, January 31, 1884.

"Jim. My name is Jim. Old Jim, if you like," he thought. The coroner had no more patience than the *Democrat* and Jim's bar mates, so Jim's other observations went unrecorded. And since others rarely interrupted his thoughts, he remembered all of it.

Christine Rush: The Neighboring Saloon

She knew Mutschler well enough. You can't have saloons next door to each other and not have any idea of the competition. She fully expected to be called to testify, and so appeared in the courtroom in a dark blue suit she made especially for the occasion.

She had talked to John Sterner that day in the back room of the saloon she ran with her husband. A Dutchman,[iv] Adolph Lang, told her that Mutschler would kill Sterner if he went in Mutschler's saloon. Lang is one of those men that can't keep nothin' to himself. Somebody told him, so of course he told everybody he saw. He's just like that.

"Sterner looked awful pale," Christine testified. "He was just sitting there, sort of hunched over. I said he should go home and just stay out of Mutschler's way."

Sterner couldn't win a fight with a jack rabbit, if it came to that. That's what she was thinking.

Christian Huntsinger: A Bystander

Among the dozens of men who found their way to Perham, Christian hoped of something new, something better offered by work to be found there. These men came when work panned out, and they left when it didn't. Huntsinger headed to

Wisconsin in the spring and had no idea that the District Court back in Minnesota was looking for him as a material witness. Held up the trial and everything for him and that blabbermouth, Adolph Lang. But he was in Mutschler's saloon that January night when Adolph Lang came huffing in, announcing "that fellow is over there in Rush's!" Everybody knew what fellow he meant and what a tinderbox Mutschler was.

"Why light the match?" Huntsinger thought.

August's brother F.A., Mrs. Mutschler and Huntsinger tried to keep him from going to Rush's and got him to sit down for a few minutes. Then he got up, he said to shut his blinds; he had to go outside to do that. Huntsinger told him, "Don't go out! Don't be so foolish."

But Mutschler went. A quick punch in the face was probably all he was looking to deliver. If Lang had kept his mouth shut, Mutschler might have put a hole through the cupboard door behind the bar, but, from what Huntsinger had heard, it wouldn't have been the first time—and he'd have recovered from that.

Will Turk

"I saw Sterner that night when he came in the [Rush's] saloon. ... I was in there when Sterner came in and I was there when Mutschler died."
—William Turk in sworn testimony, recorded in the Return of Justice on Examination, June 4, 1884.

Will Turk had been in town about two weeks, but that's long enough to know about a man like Mutschler. Turk headed to Rush's that night and hadn't been in there for more than five minutes when here comes John Sterner, looking a little wild-eyed and wobbly. Pretty soon, Mutschler showed up, asked Sterner if he'd been telling lies about him and said he ought to give him a lickin'," Turk testified at the inquest. "Then Sterner says, 'All right, come on! I'll defend myself.'"

Mutschler took a swing at him, but that blow barely touched him. Mutschler put up his hands, thinking Sterner was going to take a swing at him, but instead Sterner dropped his hands. When he brought them back up, he was holding a revolver. Mutschler swung at it and Lawrence Rush ran towards them, shouting, 'Don't shoot!' But he couldn't get there in time, and Sterner fired. Mutschler never landed a blow, and collapsed at the young man's feet, his coat on fire from the shot.

"When I let go of him, he fell backwards onto the floor; I helped him on his feet again, but just then Aaron Moses grabbed hold of him," Turk told the Court.

The blood draining from Mutschler's meaty face seemed to be pouring right onto the floor in front of Will Turk; his round, dark eyes looked up at him in bewilderment, but nobody was as bewildered as Will.

"Mutschler fell a second time, but we got him to his knees, but then laid him down on the floor, 'cause Sam Caughey said, 'Straighten him out, as he is about dead.' We laid him out and he died about two or three minutes after that."

Old Jim

Many things Old Jim knew might have been useful to the prosecution or the defense, but neither had an interest in inquiring. That was unfortunate. He knew John Sterner had told a *Weekly Journal* reporter that he felt compelled to do what he did—that it was self-defense because he knew he could not fight. He bought a Smith & Wesson specifically for the purpose.

But Jim, whose life revolved around a real medical condition, knew that Sterner's doctors suspected imagined ones in his case, concocted from worry, and Jim wondered why the prosecution didn't do anything with Sterner's admission of premeditation, which he'd made little effort to conceal.

Capt. M.E. Clapp, Esq. argued for the defense with great drama that Sterner's gun went off accidentally, wrapping a juror's hands around the gun and demonstrating how this could happen. It didn't alter the fact that Sterner illegally concealed a loaded weapon when he walked into Rush's Saloon that night, but Sterner had a sister, Mrs. E. G. Love, who had put a lot of pressure on her husband to help her brother, pushing to capitalize on a loophole that allowed someone to carry a concealed weapon if they had reason to fear bodily harm by another. Well, that was their take on it, anyway.

The Fergus Falls *Weekly Journal* played along, reporting—quite unnecessarily—that the testimony of Aaron Moses and "the oldest Rush boy" alone was enough to acquit Sterner. In fact, Moses and "the oldest Rush boy" corroborated Jim's own rendition, which would have convicted him. But Capt. Clapp, a skilled trial lawyer, cherry-picked his way through Moses' testimony and constructed a scenario in his final argument that Jim wished he could have delivered himself, even though it was a bullshit version of the truth, Jim thought.

"Mutschler was a strong, burly, healthy, quarrelsome and offensive man, while his client was a weak, inoffensive and unassuming man, suffering, still, at the time of the unfortunate affair from sickness. Mutschler was simply prepared to defend himself, while Sterner was not," Clapp said, and the *Journal* duly reported it.

"I never saw the revolver in Sterner's hand," Moses said in his initial testimony, which Jim did not doubt was true, since Moses wasn't even looking at that moment; he was looking at Jim with a smirk on his face and a beer mug raised to his lips.

"Here's to ya, J-J-Jim," he'd said.

Jim smiled back, raised his mug in a friendly toast and managed to get out, "And t-t-to you, M-M-Mr. M-m-oses," and glanced past Moses' shoulder just in time to see Sterner's hand pull the Smith & Wesson out of his pocket. Mutschler couldn't have seen the gun any more than Moses had eyes in the back of his head. Mutschler was off to Sterner's left, and Sterner pulled the gun out of his right pocket. If Mutschler could have seen it (this seemed painfully obvious to Jim!) he might not have taken that first swing.

Bottom line, that stupid Sterner wouldn't have had anything to worry about if he hadn't run to the Perham Village Council in the first place to tattle on Mutschler. People saw Mutschler's blustering as harmless, and even if he *had* threatened to burn the town down, Sterner was likely the only person who took the threat seriously. Plenty of people heard about it, but nobody else was compelled to report it.

Jim had heard just how strapped Mutschler really was. The Village Council had already ordered Mutschler to pay a judgment large enough to compromise his liquor supply—that was concerning a different matter—so when Sterner ratted on Mutschler, he was threatening to strip the man of his livelihood.

The council didn't find sufficient evidence to arrest Mutschler, but the man—pushed to the brink as he was—would not let such an affront rest. So, yes, when you corner an angry creature, you must be prepared for an attack. But a gun? To avoid a black eye and a couple of cracked ribs? Even Jim was vaguely amused by the shooter's cowardice. If Sterner felt vulnerable, it was his own fault. Jim knew better than to antagonize a man like Mutschler. Sterner was just an ass, and now found himself in the embarrassing position of playing on his weaknesses and requiring the pleas of a woman to save him. Jim had never stooped that low.

The consensus in the courtroom as the jury filed out to deliberate was unfavorable to the prisoner. Jim, however, fully expected that the jury would not convict. They're not supposed to talk, but they do. Opinions percolate long before the judge gives his final instructions. Their whispered comments to each other couldn't have been heard by the audience or even the attorneys seated next to the jury box. But as they didn't cover their mouths, Jim didn't need to hear them.

Whether or not any of this could have changed the outcome for John Sterner is another matter. Public sentiments buoyed by Mr. Love's subtle courting of those sentiments ... well, that's a powerful force for a member of the jury to face, once the trial closes and he returns to the society on which his own livelihood rests.

One way or another, Sterner wouldn't face the gallows. Ol' Jim couldn't help but wonder, though, what the attorneys might have done with the information he could have provided. But hell ... if they couldn't figure it out on their own, Jim was not about to come forward, disrupt the course of "justice," and set himself up for more ridicule. It would get around, and the paper would joke about that, too. Damn 'em all.

The trial of John C. Sterner for the murder of Anton Mutschler of Perham was held in the district court at Fergus Falls, Otter Tail County, before Judge Collins. ... The prisoner's plea of defense was self-protection ... The Jury brought in a verdict of not guilty and the prisoner on being dismissed, took the train for Iowa. — Perham *Bulletin,* June 12, 1884.

Sure enough, the German cadre warned Deputy Butler to leave town within 24 hours of the "not guilty" verdict, but this time, Butler was ready, swearing in five more deputies, "all husky lumberjacks who were fairly itching for hostilities to begin," a Fergus Falls *Daily Journal* story years later said. Heavily armed, they patrolled the streets two-by-two and "the mob spirit finally subsided."

9. The Pigs and a Plow, October 1885

HOMESTEAD SHOOTING: STORY OF THE KILLING OF PAUL
KOERNER AS TOLD AT THE CORONER'S INQUEST.

A SAD TRAGEDY WHICH RESULTED FROM A TRIFLING
MATTER—THE PIGS AND THE PLOW.

AUGUST LEOPOLD POSER BOUND OVER TO THE GRAND
JURY WHICH MEETS IN NOVEMBER.

A woman in calico dress and sunbonnet, a man in homespun clothes, worn boots and a large-brimmed hat, that's a common picture of European pioneers. The young children are small clones of their parents. They ride in a wagon piled with belongings that are pulled by a team of oxen.

The Posers may be the closest to this scenario—two brothers, their wives and small children, traveling with a friend. Desperately poor, they couldn't have been more ordinary. No one among them could afford the basic requirements to operate a farm alone, so they shared one wagon, a team of oxen, and a plow. This gave them a chance, at least, to make a go of it on the last available—and least desirable—land in the northeast corner of Otter Tail County, far from the rich prairie soil to the southwest.

The Posers were isolated, but they survived, and their families took root in the very place they homesteaded—all except the one non-family member in their little group. Extreme poverty can diminish even the most resilient souls, and bickering is an inevitable release from the exhaustion and unraveling that accompanies relentless, demanding work, especially for the one among them who had no wife or family, much less his own home.

> Even so, the spats were not just an emotional response. In truth, there was only so much time to complete field work and harvest a garden. This required compromises and sharing so they would all have enough to eat through the long winter.

Coroner Bedford returned Sunday morning from Perham, where he went to hold an inquest over the remains of Paul Koerner, who was shot by Paul (sic) Leopold Poser, according to the doctor's statement Homestead is not a very good place for holding inquests. He was informed that he could not get a jury in the town, so he impaneled the jury in Perham and taking two days' provisions started for the site of the shooting, sixteen miles distant, over the poorest roads and roughest country in the county. Three teams were necessary to convey the jury, provisions and other necessaries. A coffin was also taken along. —Fergus Falls *Weekly Journal,* October 22, 1885.

The Posers Make Their Way to Homestead Township, Spring 1884

The women's dress and the men's trousers were stiff with the oil, pollen, dirt, and debris from weeks of travel. Her hands clicked the knitting needles in a frantic rhythm to complete another pair of socks, another hat, mittens, or scarf. There were two brothers, Charles and August Poser; their wives, Agnes and Frances, respectively; their little children; and Paul Koerner, a single man and Charles' friend. Paul would share in their labors, and have the benefit of a woman's cooking, the camaraderie of Charles and his brother, a roof over his head. Paul was hot tempered, but he was German, and that's what counted.

The woman named Agnes, whose round face poked out from her bonnet, had full cheeks that made her look much too young to be the mother of three. She turned now and then to admire her husband August's broad back. He rarely sat on the wagon's seat with her; walking beside the oxen, hollering "gee!" and "haw!" to direct their movement forward, all the while calculating how much farther they must go before stopping for the night. It wasn't possible to travel fast with the kinder. Five-year-old Arno got to walk beside the wagon with his Papa or Paul. Haitwick, at barely four years old, was a quick little girl, and got a swat on her behind if she didn't stay within sight of her Papa. Walter was just a toddler and crawled among the family's few belongings packed tightly in the wagon.

Homestead Township, Otter Tail County, October 1885

The Poser family had nothing, so there was nothing to lose by trying to make a living someplace else. They had found land still available in the northeast corner of Otter Tail County. It was rocky and wooded, but they would pile rocks and fell trees until every inch of it yielded and provided for their needs. They knew how to work hard, and they would make that pale soil littered with pebbles turn out a crop, or at least hay enough to feed some decent Holsteins. Let the rest of the county chase after wheat.

"They'll all need milk, butter and cheese!" Agnes would declare almost daily. Actually, their farm was no match for the wheat fields that rolled with no effort across the plains west and south of Fergus Falls. Agnes was not dissuaded. "*Wir werden es tun!*" she'd say. "We Germans can do it!"

Mid-October. Each brother had a piece of land and a cabin just one-half mile apart. August owned the wagon, Charles owned the oxen, and Paul pitched in for a plow with Charles. Their survival depended on making it work—and, although their shared ownership had been trying, they were close to harvesting the last of what was to be had before they must turn the earth back over to the long, Minnesota winter. Each had cleared and planted a small feed plot and garden.

For Paul, having to share a house was a daily reminder of how little he claimed in this world. His temper flared often. Charles had to take Paul's part sometimes; he had to live with him, after all. August knew this and tried to let things go.

Maybe the arrangement worked in part because they were so exhausted that there was no energy left to quarrel.

... The Posers, who were very poor, used their things in common, and of the personal effects involved in the tragedy, August owned the wagon, Charles the oxen, and Charles and Koerner the plow. Up to last Monday there had never been any trouble of any kind. —Fergus Falls *Weekly Journal*, October 22, 1885.

Agnes Poser

Sundays should have been their day of rest, but there was wood to split and stack, the garden to turn over, and a thousand other things before the snow came and the work of a new season took over. But when both were feeling poorly that Sunday, they had no choice but to feed the animals and collapse on the straw bed in the corner of their little cabin. The children were sent to stay with Frances.

The next day, Agnes set out to fetch the oxen from Charles' place. Some of her pigs followed her, but they followed her everywhere, especially when she was carrying a bucket, and she thought nothing of it. It was a crisp, dry October day, the kind that assured you the whole day to work. The sun was warm; the poplar trees' golden leaves brightened the woods nearby. They had so little, but that day Agnes felt like she had everything she needed as she walked across the furrows to Charles' and Frances' place.

She was unprepared for what awaited her. Paul had the oxen hitched to the wagon. "You had the plow Sunday, so plow," he told her. He propped one elbow on the wagon like he owned it himself, which he did not. Agnes was not going to be pushed around so easily, though.

"We were sick," she told him. "We couldn't plow."

Paul just smirked at her, grabbed the switch and pointed the oxen toward August and Agnes' place. She was stunned as the wagon lurched onto the rutted path. There was nothing to do but follow.

By the time she reached their shed, August had the oxen unhitched. Paul had a switch raised behind him, but before he could lash out at August, Paul was on the ground with August's hands latched around his throat. She cared little about Paul at that moment, but she was not about to be part of his murder. "Let him up, let him up!" she screamed.

More's the pity. Paul was no sooner on his feet than he was swinging at her! The startled woman fell back into the dirt, her skirt flew up over her knees, and she grabbed a corner of it to wipe her bleeding nose. August appeared from the cabin with his shotgun and Agnes scrambled to get out of the way.

"Shoot! Coward! Dog!" Paul shouted at him, but August didn't shoot.

Paul picked up a rock as big as his fist and hurled it at August, but it missed. The shotgun was still pointed at the back of Paul's head as he called to the oxen to drive them out of the yard and back toward Charles' place. When August finally lowered the gun, Agnes stumbled to her feet and followed his gesture to get the wagon into the shed, her heart beating as fast as a bird's.

"Go get your pigs, or you'll never see them again," August told her, but she was terrified to face Paul alone, so her husband followed her.

"Go away!" Paul hollered at her. Agnes glanced back at August, who had paused on the neighbor, Mr. Moke's, property, so he couldn't be accused of trespassing.

"I'll go as soon as I have my pigs," she called back to Paul, her voice shaking as she called to the pigs and rattled the bucket filled with food scraps. But they wouldn't come!

Paul spotted August in Moke's grove and leaped across the yard with his pitchfork, charging toward August, shrieking "Shoot! … Coward! … Dog!" August kept backing up, but soon he would be right next to Mr. Moke's house, and what had they to do with any of this?

Frances burst through the door, her apron crumpled in her hands, pleading, "Don't stab! Don't shoot!" but it was too late for the thought in the barrel of the gun and the movement of the man holding it. The gun fired. Paul dropped the pitchfork, clutched his arm and fell in a stumbling gait through the doorway.

Agnes stood, frozen in the spot. "Keep the pigs, Frances. Just keep them! You can pay me later." That was all she could get out.

"No," Frances answered, in a voice Agnes and never heard from her. "I have enough trouble with my own. Keep your own goddam pigs!"

Paul's arm sprouted blood like a fountain when he dashed headlong past Agnes into the house. All she could think about was her children skipping alongside Paul as they grasped at another mile of the trail that would lead them all to a better life. "You're one of us!" she cried. "Or you were!"

"Aggie!" August called out to her. "Get home now!" And she took her head out of the storybook she'd concocted and followed her husband—her protector, her life, really—across the small strip of bumpy furrows that separated them from the only connection left to their lives in Germany. His brother!

Mr. Moke went to dress Paul's wound with arnica. But Paul was lightheaded, and his face had a yellow cast. Moke was alarmed and sent August to fetch Dr. Bertholdt in the middle of the night. The doctor thought it was a flesh wound, too; he didn't realize that Paul's arm was in pieces inside, and it was killing him. By Thursday afternoon, he was dead.

The Posers do not seem to realize that anything uncommon has happened and they expected August back home Saturday night. He was taken before Justice C.D.C. Williams, of Perham, and it is expected that he will be brought in to-morrow morning by [Deputy] Sheriff Butler. The Posers are very poor and August's family, consisting of a wife and four children, were almost destitute. —Fergus Falls *Weekly Journal*, October 22, 1885.

In District Court
7th Judicial District
November 1885
The State of Minnesota, AGAINST August Leopold Poser

August Leopold Poser is accused by the Grand Jury of the County of Otter Tail, in the State of Minnesota, by this indictment of the crime of Manslaughter in the Second degree Committed as follow: The said August Leopold Poser on the 12th day of October A.D. 1885 at the town of Homestead in the said County of Otter Tail and State of Minnesota feloniously killed Paul Koerner in the heat of passion, upon sudden provocation, intuitively, but without premeditation, and not under such circumstances as to constitute excusable or justifiable homicide, but shooting him with a gun …

Frances and Charles Poser

"Self-defense." Charles said. "The jury said that."

"And what do you say?" Frances asked.

"Well, that's the law. So be it."

Frances turned to face him. She needed to see something on his face that she could depend on for their future. "Your brother is home, so … *Das ist gut*, yah?"

"It's good? There were three of us. Now there are two," he said. He turned his back on her and paused before he pulled on his coat, heavy mittens, and cap, swung the door open and stepped into the cold.

Frances waited a moment before pushing the door closed. The cold air was bracing and forced her to move, pulling her woolen shawl tighter around her shoulders. Winter was just beginning.

August Poser was charged; his wife was not charged, but (once again) there was no conviction and punishment. One could make the argument that the public good was better served by letting the perpetrator go home to take care of his family. He certainly wasn't a threat to anybody else. Besides, it appears that neither the authorities nor the general populace cared enough about people this far down the rungs of the societal ladder to pursue another conclusion.

The Fergus Falls *Weekly Journal* called it *"a sad tragedy which resulted from a trifling matter—the pigs and the plow."* But these were not trifling for families living so close to the edge. To add to the indignity, the authorities had whined about the difficulties entailed in getting to the scene of the crime, which was reported in some detail in the Fergus Falls *Journal.* Three years later a report concerning a shooting in neighboring Becker County recalled the Poser incident in a similar tone of condescension.

The killing of Kohler by Adams north of Perham is quite similar to the killing of Koerner by Poser in the town of Homestead, only a short distance away. A human life in that section has never been regarded as anything sacred, and a neighborhood row is generally sufficient cause for murder. Fortunately this case is just over the Becker county line so that it cannot be charged up to Otter Tail. —Fergus Falls *Weekly Journal,* October 20, 1887.

10. The Divorce Client, Winter 1886

The man who commits a crime while intoxicated is equally guilty with a sober man committing the same offense, as he is responsible for the act of getting drunk. … if a plea of drunkenness were allowed as an excuse for crime, all an intending lawbreaker need to do would be to fill himself with bad whiskey before undertaking such offences against law as he might choose to commit. —The Democrat, January 17, 1884.

A bout two years after the *Democrat* printed its condemnation of the intoxication defense, its liberal point of view had not made much headway in Otter Tail County, illustrated by the verdict in the shooting of Peter Smith by Bernard (Barney) Kempfer in the village of Elizabeth. At the time, the law did not recognize intoxication as a defense by itself, but it could be used to raise questions concerning *intent.* Public opinion, however, disregarded this finer point—and it was the public who would decide the fate of a man who had been drunk the better part of a year.

B.O. KEMPFER SHOOTS ATTORNEY P.N. SMITH AT ELIZABETH THIS NOON WITH POSSIBLY FATAL RESULTS

The trouble which led to the shooting grew out of a divorce suit, which is now pending before Judge Baxter, in which Mrs. Kempfer is trying to secure a divorce from Kempfer, and the custody of the children, on the grounds of drunkenness and inhuman treatment. The divorce has been granted, and the matter of the custody of the children had not been decided … It is believed that Kempfer is delirious from continued drinking and was not sane when the shooting occurred. —Fergus Falls *Daily Journal,* February 2, 1886.

But Barney Kempfer did not invoke the drunkenness plea in his 1886 murder trial, and was, in fact, bent on representing himself as basically sober when the crime was committed. Yet Barney's slide into alcoholism was common knowledge and had even cost him a job as Elizabeth's town clerk at one time. His threats against several people, including Peter Smith, his wife's lawyer in her divorce proceedings, were also well known. But Kempfer still had his allies, and Peter Smith hadn't helped himself much with his own dicey reputation.

One of the earliest pioneers, Smith had no compunctions about trying his hand at any profession, regardless of his lack of preparation. Veterinary medicine, insurance sales and law all had their turns. His legal skills and his penchant for settling disagreements with his fists prompted open derision in newspaper reports on his various scuffles.

PETER N. SMITH ADMITTED BEHIND THE BARS

We think we have heretofore mentioned that the chrysalis doctor—P.N. Smith—was studying the science of law. Well, last fall Peter N. was admitted to the bar to practice in the district court. But business did not flow in as rapidly as he had fondly hoped. … At a dance at Burau's hotel [in Elizabethtown] Christmas night Peter got into a row with Rudolph Niggeler and one of the Burau boys and pulled a revolver and threatened to "let daylight through them." For this little diversion he was arrested …[and] it was taken before Justice Geo. F. Cowing. It appeared to the justice that it was only a lack of courage that prevented Peter's giving the coroner a job, bound the young man over in the sum of $500 to appear at the District Court, or failing to get the necessary bonds, the Sheriff was instructed to gently admit him behind the bars. Medbury [an unknown participant] says his being bound over was wholly due to the fact that he plead his own case instead of getting some one who knew something about law to attend to it for him. —The Advocate, December 30, 1874.

Mrs. Kempfer Hires Peter N. Smith, Esq., Late 1885

Light footfalls on the steps gave her away. She walked slowly, hesitating often, and stopped in front of his door. A frightened woman. A divorce? He didn't like family law, but he was in no position to turn down work—and he was too keenly aware of the violence that invaded some homes. He pictured her frozen with her hand on the knocker, just below his nameplate, "Peter M. Smith, Esq., Attorney at Law," or standing by the newel post transfixed above the stairs, crumpling and uncrumpling a white handkerchief trimmed with tatting. It would be her best one. This was as close as she came to going out, other than church, when her husband would allow it—and if she was presentable enough.

He even had a good idea about which frightened woman it might be. Hans, Herman Burau's bartender, had tossed him a tip about a week ago over a late afternoon beer in Burau's saloon. It was no surprise. Barney Kempfer's wife. There was a storm raging inside that man, fueled by uncontrolled drinking.

Mrs. Kempfer … Alice … had her hands full with two boys so close in age they looked like twins. Bernard Jr. and Francis, but they called them Bernie and Frankie. They had to be about ten or eleven now, at least, and with their father's rants blaming everyone but himself for his fall from grace, and his daily raging against their mother, they were spiraling out of control. The Kempfers had a girl, too, who was a little older than Smith's own daughter.

Barney was not going to take this quietly. The members of the Otter Tail County Bar would find a pretext to demean Smith for taking on such a case; a woman belonged with her husband, they would say. But Peter M. Smith, Esq. really didn't give a damn what they thought, and that was the illustrious county bar's problem with him.

She didn't knock. She just opened the door and quickly shut it again behind her. A hanky wrinkled with its recent abuse, was poised in front of her mouth, a missing front tooth still visible behind it. A bit of powder couldn't hide the pale grayish yellow tint around her left eye, the leftovers from a previous attack.

"Please, sit down," Peter told her, and she complied. "Can I help you?"

She didn't answer but cleared her throat.

"A glass of water?" He didn't wait for an answer and brought her the water.

"Thank you," she said at last, and took a sip. "I need a divorce from Barney."

And the sobs began. She had no money of her own ... she couldn't pay him yet ... but Barney had a little money ... she could pay him from that. She'd do anything if he would just help her ...

Of course, he would help her. No one else would, he figured; Barney still had some influence and friends enough. And he happened to know that Barney had a little money, so yes, he'd get paid. He prepared a simple document for her to sign, which she did without looking at even the first "whereas." He asked her if she would be able to get home all right and opened the door for her. The sweep of her skirt and heavy winter underskirts rustled in waves as she descended the stairs—soft crinkles with the tiny click of her high-button boots. She stopped near the last step, looked up, and called out in something like a whisper and a gasp, "Thank you!"

In Justice Court: The Preliminary Examination of B.O. Kempfer for the Shooting of P.N. Smith: *Arnold Hartmann called. I live in Elizabeth; am a blacksmith ... His [Kempfer's] wife stopped at my place after the divorce suit began; I had conversations with Kempfer in reference to Smith; it was in Herman Bureau's saloon on Monday, Feb. 1, the day before the shooting; I went in with John Rufer.* —Fergus Falls *Daily Journal*, February 8, 1886.

It is believed that Kempfer is delirious from continued drinking, and was not sane when the shooting occurred. —Fergus Falls *Daily Journal*, *February 2, 1886.*

Hans Field the Bartender, February 2, 1886

At more than six feet tall, Hans Field towered over most of Herman Burau's saloon customers, and with his dusty red hair, sitting like a cap on top of his long, narrow face and freckled ears he had the look of a pileated woodpecker. His scraggly beard and dour expression made him look older than his twenty-two years. One couldn't help but wonder if that look would just sit there on the young Norwegian's face right through old age. Burau liked him, as it was useful to have an imposing young fellow serving behind the bar. But he was a quiet sort, too. And agreeable.

Pete Smith was one of those fellows who could figure out how to make a buck doing just about anything. He always livened up the saloon when he stopped by, which was most days. Hans got the sense that it was at least part business with him. Burau's was where everybody came when they were done working. But Mr. Smith? Hans had watched him pick up business of all kinds in the saloon—lawyering, insurance, dickering about something he was "willing to part with"—even doctoring. Oh, he could work it all! Pete Smith was scrappy like that.

"But he ain't a boot licker, *nei, han er ikke*," Hans would say. No, he's not. He liked him, but he knew that people either liked Pete or they didn't. He careened through life, swinging his fists a little too easily. But Hans never saw Pete do anything to hurt anybody, lest they had it coming.

That was the way with Barney Kempfer that day. He came in already full as a tick. Now Pete, he was a careful drinker. Kept his head about him, except on special occasions, like holidays, when things would get a bit rowdier. But on this day, he'd come in to collect the money for an insurance premium from Mr. Burau: $31.50.

"You put on 50-cents for spending money," Burau said.

Pete gave a little laugh and said, "All right, you treat, then."

Hans' woodpecker head bobbed. He didn't quite manage a smile, though.

There was only Hans and Mr. Burau, a farmer named Becker and Barney in the place at first; a few others showed up later. Hans put up what they ordered, but Barney, who'd just come in, said he didn't want anything. "I won't drink with a two-faced man," Barney says.

"Who do you mean by that?" Pete asks.

"You're the son-of-a-bitch I mean." Barney says, and just keeps up with the foul-mouth talk.

Hans was putting water in the punch on the woodstove in the middle of the room, when Pete had had enough and made his move. Barney was sitting in the corner chair when Pete bare fisted him in the face, knocked him to the floor, and sent the chair flying. Hans thought that might be the end of it, since Barney was in no condition for a proper fight, but Pete hit him again, and then kicked him hard in the gut.

"Smith, what are you doing?" Burau hollered and raced over to pull Pete off Barney, but by then the shooting started.

That first shot hit Pete—Hans heard a sharp *thwmp* and saw Pete's jacket flare up in smoke with the hit. There was another and at least one more after that, but Hans wasn't counting; he wanted safety. The third shot—or there might have been a fourth—missed, he was sure. It pinged off the doorframe, and Hans leaped across the room and dove over the top and behind the bar. Only one shot missed anyway, which Hans couldn't figure, since when he looked again, Pete continued pounding Barney.

Burau finally got Barney's revolver away, but then Pete pulled out his revolver, crawled behind the stove and fired. But it didn't go off! Barney got on his feet and made a break for the front door, but Pete, dripping blood like a son-of-a-gun, caught up with him between the saloon and the storm doors on the outside. Barney got Pete's revolver away and by that time, Pete was bent over at the waist with his left arm clutching his right arm around his gut.

Pete didn't make another sound. The sudden quiet was distressing—even worse than all the ruckus. Then Pete fell against the outside storm door with a crash that startled Hans, who ran to the door. Pete was on his feet, though, heading towards his house two blocks away. Across the street, Barney was running towards his house, too.

Hans looked from Pete to Mr. Burau, then back to Barney, just in time to see a little kid—one of Barney's boys—tearing down the street towards his papa. Bernie or Frankie; he couldn't tell those two apart. When Barney wobbled, dropped to one knee and looked back towards Pete, who was dragging himself when he couldn't walk, the boy snatched the gun from somewhere (did Burau just throw it in the street?) and took off with it. Burau said nothing, nobody found it, and the kid wouldn't tell. Hans suspected that Bernie and Frankie both knew.

Alice Kempfer

Yes, the boys both knew. So did I. The boys grew up knowing how to trick their Pa, and they were clever about it. What with Barney slapping them around—that was on a good day—or taking them to the woodshed for a switch on a worse one ... well, they knew how to steer clear when the time called for it. And this I know: not one of us would ever reveal the location of that gun. I told them it was the right thing to do, which is all they needed to hear.

... Dr. W. C. Bedford went to the scene of the affray. An examination was made of the wounds and the bullet was extricated from the one in the shoulder. The wound in the abdomen has been probed, but the bullet has not been found, and it will prove fatal. Smith showed wonderful grit and endurance. He made a full statement of the affair and calmly contemplated the fatal result. To-day he has been sinking and made his will. Smith has a wife and three bright children, the oldest of which is about twelve. — Fergus Falls *Daily Journal*, February 9, 1886.

Mr. Smith died Saturday afternoon the sixth of February. Four days it took him. I barely ate or slept that whole week. My Mary took over the household chores, and kept the boys in line, too. She told 'em they better keep that stove stoked or they'd freeze, starve or both. Never was I so grateful to have a girl old enough to take on the house chores. Truth is—for Mary, anyways—household chores seemed like nothing when Barney wasn't around. There was a lightness about her, knowing he was locked up. I didn't know how wonderful it would be to have him gone. But when Mr. Smith died, I was all jumbled inside with no one to show it to. I did my best to keep my head up, but since our private matters would come out in a public trial for the whole county to know, I was much confused. How was I supposed to act?

Barney made bail and was out until the trial in May. He stayed with friends who tried to tell us he meant no harm, but I knew better. If he could stay sober, though, we'd all live through it. For now. Staying sober would also help him beat the charge, and that was the most terrifying thought of all. If he won, then what?

... The defendant, a man of medium height, dressed in a full suit of dark blue came into the courtroom and took his seat at the table beside his counsel, Messrs. Rawson and Houpt. He wears a full beard, and but for a streak of grey, it would be a full, clear black. He appears calm, except that he occasionally uses his handkerchief to wipe perspiration from his face and the palms of his hands. —Fergus Falls *Weekly Journal*, June 10, 1886.

Barney Kempfer Takes the Stand, Early June 1886

Dr. McLean provided the jury with an account of Barney Kempfer's injuries ... his face was bruised, his eye swollen shut and bones in his nose had been broken. But Kempfer recovered and was called as the key witness for the defense.

"I have been keeping hotel part of the time and practicing as a veterinary surgeon," he told the court. He had also been a Justice of the Peace in Elizabeth and had heard legal issues brought by the man he shot to death in Burau's Saloon.

"I first knew Smith in July of 1879," Kempfer said. "Relations have always been friendly up to last August; on my part this feeling has been friendly since." Just about everybody in the courtroom, including Dr. McLean, wore a smirk after that line 'a bull.

There was a lawsuit in that month, Kempfer admitted that he had decided. It didn't go Smith's way and Smith was livid.

"'If you ever get in my way,' Smith said, 'I'll fill you half full of lead, and you'll have a worse disease than delirium tremens!'"

"I told him, 'You are a son-of-a-bitch,' but I said it in a moderate tone."

The defendant stopped to wipe perspiration with his handkerchief, cleared his throat and looked up, sitting upright and stock still, but for his hands, still carefully wiping the palms of his hands. The observers took the short pause in his testimony to adjust in their seats; boots scraped across the plank floor and ladies' underskirts rustled. Barney seemed not to notice the presence of anyone.

"He gave me a terrible blow; I fell backward; I received several more blows." Barney paused again, placed his handkerchief against his nose and sniffed. "I think he kicked me ... I'm ... not certain. Smith said, 'God damn, you! I'll murder you!' After that, I saw him reach back for his hip pocket ... then I shot him."

The benches in the jury box creaked as the men leaned back and forth whispering comments to each other.

"I never carried it," Barney said. "I kept it in my trunk at home. But I was going that day with some others to see the Ice Palace in St. Paul. I took it to carry with me. He drew his revolver before he got away. There was smoke before me, and I thought he had shot me; I felt ... pain. Smith got away from me. Burau asked for my revolver, and I gave it to him. I went a few feet on my hands and knees, then I got up. Smith followed me, swearing at me, and snapped his revolver. But I got it away from him and put it in my pocket."

Kempfer patted the pocket of his suit jacket, as if to solidify the remark. "I brought it to Fergus and gave it to the sheriff."

A few of the jurors nodded and one even smiled weakly. It was hard to know if that was because he approved, or just didn't believe Kempfer's contradictory testimony. A gun supposedly disappeared with his son. So, whose gun is he talking about? In the box, throats were cleared, arms were crossed. Still Barney Kempfer seemed oblivious of the jury. What he wanted was a drink.

C.L. Lewis, county attorney, summed up the case for the state ... He argued the case first under the assumption that Kempfer acted under a deliberate and carefully formed intent to kill Smith... Mr. Rawson for the defense claimed the act of Kempfer was done purely and simply in self-defense, after he saw Smith reaching to draw a weapon, and what any man would have done under the circumstances. ... The jury was out about two hours, and then returned with a verdict of not guilty of the indictment as charged, and the prisoner was set at liberty. —Fergus Falls *Weekly Journal,* June 10, 1886.

Smith deserved his notoriety, but he did at least one thing right: he represented Alice Kempfer. It cost him his life, but it may very well have saved hers. Even so, this crime was never really about Pete Smith; it was about Barney Kempfer's deeply personal problems. Drinking had cost him his prestige in the community and his career in public service. It was about to cost him his family, too.

As the one who filed for divorce, Alice got in the first "punch" this time, and she would get custody of their three children, as well as a decent settlement of $425. Just like thousands of women, before or since, who feel trapped and fear for their lives, Alice had suffered all the abuse she was going to take.

For a woman in 1885 in a small, remote village on the edge of the frontier to take the step and file for divorce … that was extraordinary and courageous— and Barney knew it. In the end, he just looked small.

11. Making Room for Better People, August 12, 1886

MURDER AND SUICIDE.

WILSON, A COOK IN LULU HARRIS' BAGNIE, SHOOTS HER
FATALLY AT 2 P. M. TO-DAY.

HE THEN TAKES LAUDANUM AND MORPHINE AND ROWS
OUT ON THE LAKE TO DIE.

About 2 o'clock this afternoon Lulu Harris who keeps the house of ill repute out on the Elizabeth Road, quarreled with her cook, an old man named Wilson, who fired five shots at her with a 45-calibre revolver. All the shots took effect... and she has since died from the wounds. Wilson at once took a rowboat and went out on the lake; when he was called to come in he answered that he had taken laudanum and that the boat should be his coffin. ... Wilson is still out in the middle of the lake and the officers are unable to get him as he has the only boat. LATER... The report that Miss Harris was dead was premature. She was living at last accounts but was liable to die at any moment. —Fergus Falls *Weekly Journal,* August 12, 1886 [v]

Other than Lillie Field, only one woman is among the victims. The proprietor of a brothel, she called herself Lulu (or Lou) Harris; even on her death bed, she would not reveal her real name. It was not a customer or one of her "inmates," as they called the women working there, who shot her on that balmy August afternoon. It was a man known by various names, including Ned (or Nick) Wilson, identified as her cook and "runner." He identified himself as her husband. She did not agree. She had, of late, preferred a man named Baker, a lot younger than Ned, and not addicted to opium.

Ned wouldn't have had much trouble getting his hands on the drug, as it was legal in the U.S. Opium derivatives were often used in non-prescription "tonics," but, as an addict, Ned's use would have been more hard-core—an "opium eater"—ingesting the gummy substance or "wad" in its more elemental form.

But not Lulu. Not a user, much less an addict. She was also known to conduct herself in public "with becoming propriety," a news report said, but the county was still not going to look the other way regarding her profession, so in October 1885, it indicted her for "keeping a house of ill fame" in Fergus Falls and kicked her out of town. She spent the next few months in Aitken 130 miles to the east but bought a house in Fergus Falls the next spring and stayed there until she was "discovered" and got kicked out again.

It's not clear when she had lived in a house off the Elizabeth Road previously, but she knew the house and must have had an arrangement with the man from St. Louis who owned it, because that's where she landed—right in between the tiny village of Elizabeth and Fergus Falls, convenient for area clients, but less convenient for law enforcement.

Lulu Harris, August 12, 1886

When Lulu Harris returned to Fergus Falls after the winter of 1885-86 in Aitken, Minnesota, she brought with her a new man named Baker, much to the ire of the older Ned Wilson. Ned was an opium–eating bloodsucker who thought he owned her, having met her in her childhood home in Canada and seduced her at age twenty-two, then setting her on the path that became her life's work. His promises to her had dissipated along with any ambition he once had.

Baker, on the other hand, was dashing in a striped suit of English cut, with wavy brown hair and a perpetual smile. Clean shaven, too. He was younger than her, but nobody could have guessed. She was no fool; she took care of her good looks and took advantage of her diminutive size. Lulu could barely make five feet in her dress boots. She let her blazing mass of curly, amber-colored hair trail in bright curls down her back. A contrasting sash accentuated her tiny waist.

Baker tolerated Ned's presence in the house, since age, opium or Lulu's temper was bound to do him in soon enough. Occasionally useful as a cook or a runner, he was not to be relied upon, given his romance with opium. Ned was mostly just irrelevant.

When Fergus Falls' lawmen bowed to pressure to eliminate the blight of her disreputable presence in that town, she returned to a house she knew near the relative torpor of Elizabeth. The county's silly indictment for selling a pint of beer without a license was a needless kick in the arse, given she'd already been "removed." Damn their two-faced twaddle. Plenty of them would find their way to her place, regardless.

It had been a slow week, what with field work on the upswing again after small grain harvest. Farmers and laborers hadn't collected on grain sales yet, and local merchants, used to extending credit, wouldn't get paid until the farmers did. Nobody spent money this time of year; they were too busy making it.

Lulu Harris paid Fannie Grant and Annie Wilkie and sent them off to town for the rest of the day. She longed to have the house all to herself—a rarity in her line of work—with nothing to do but tidy up her own boudoir, or lounge on the wide porch with a sarsaparilla. She'd open up all the heavy curtains that afforded her customers the privacy they required and let the late summer sun send rosy shafts of light through the red, glass-beaded lamp shades.

And it would be quiet. Nothing but a couple of crickets chirping in the kitchen to disturb her peace. But Ned hadn't accompanied the girls to town, and so she had to deal with his hovering and badgering, his lewd comments and incessant demands for her favors.

"C'mon, Lou," he said, his foul breath pouring across her face. "The girls are gone … it's just you and me," and reached under her skirt. "You're my wife, you know, as much as any woman who done it up proper in a church."

"I'm not your wife or your woman," she fired back. "I'm your fucking caretaker, you worthless shit pile!" She took one look at his huge pupils, whirled around and seated herself at a table in the parlor.

"It's your fancy man, isn't it," he growled, his eyes struggling to see her against the blinding sun that sliced across the room.

"I'll pay you through the end of the month if you'll leave. If not, I'll write to a lawyer who will make you leave," she said and pulled paper, pen and ink within reach. When she looked up, Ned had a revolver leveled at her head.

In less than a breath, her hands shot up to her face, but the gun exploded, shattering her wrist. Lulu bolted from the chair, hurled herself into her room, just behind the parlor, and locked the door. Ned flung his torso against the door, broke it down, and took four more shots, every one hitting her and she crumpled.

Ned Wilson

Ned had quite a stash. He'd prepared to be stuck in a house on the edge of the prairie or hotfoot it over the border into the Dakotas. Nobody bothered to chase anybody across that nothingness. But why … bother? Just rid the world of that nasty little woman, pop a load of hop and float into the great beyond in a glorious mother of all highs. Or he could save a bullet for himself and go for certitude. That's it. There … yes. That's what he'd do.

Except he used all the bullets on her. Fortunately, he had a Plan B, and he set about ingesting most of the dope he had left. It wasn't enough. In fact, he was still capable of climbing into the little rowboat pulled up in the weeds and getting himself out into the pond by the house. To what end, he wasn't sure, until his seriously taxed eyes, with the sun glaring on the reedy shoreline, fell on a good-sized rock. There was a piece of rope lying in the bottom of the boat, which he tied around the rock, with the purpose of tying the other end of the rope around his ankle, once he'd found a part of the little lake deep enough to drown a man his size. He was thrilled to have gotten himself thus far! She was dead, and he suspended in euphoria, with a lovely means of joining this world and the next well within his grasp. So, he paddled out.

The next five hours were spent drifting about the pond talking to anybody who happened along. He was perfectly safe, as he had the only boat. He could say what he liked and, for a time, enjoy the exquisite lump of time's passage that belonged to him alone. He had taken charge! That little cherry was silenced, and her fancy man could be distraught for a time and go on to other conquests. He had won the day! So, he popped another little wad of hop. He hadn't known such elation since he'd first stripped the camisole and pantaloons off that little woman, but when that was not available to him, he could still take comfort in his wad—a safety net, comfort, resolution for all his dilemmas. A sober person did not have the capacity to understand. He hated sobriety. This, though, was alarmingly wonderful to him, on that sunny, summer afternoon. He was basking indeed.

Then Sheriff Brandenburg showed up, that little shit with the dour expression and monstrosity on his lip that he no doubt called a moustache. What a wretched little man, he thought. No sense of humor at all.

"I'm jumping in, when I'm good and ready!" Ned called back to shore. Save the county the expense of chasing the perfectly obvious. It made him laugh out loud, which carried across the water to shore on this windless day.

Brandenburg sent to town for a boat, and in the meantime, Ned took a leisurely row around the pond. When Billy Colvert and another man showed up with a boat and began to row furiously toward him, Ned at last dipped in an oar to test the depth of the water, tied the rock to his ankles and hopped overboard. But the rope was tied too loosely and easily worked its way off his ankles in the tangle of bulrushes, sending Ned to the surface. Since drowning was not going according to plan, he attempted to reach his little boat, which responded to the waves Ned's plunge had created, and was rocking, as one would expect, away from Ned. He couldn't reach it and before his rescuers could reach him, Ned had tangled himself in the weedy thatch and sunk for good.

When he fled, Lulu had clawed at the heavy quilt on the bed to pull herself off the floor. The effort was enormous—and pointless—but the dying woman was determined to attain whatever comfort she could. And she waited. Three hours passed before Annie and Fannie returned from town. They summoned Dr. Duncan immediately, who extracted all but one of the bullets, and attempted to alleviate her suffering, but the doctor had already determined that her injuries would be fatal. She lingered until 4:00 a.m. the next morning.

Among the striking things about the story is the muted response to her death compared to the more sensationalized reports typical of other murders. What do you do when tragedy strikes a place like Lulu Harris'? It was awkward, but protocol was followed. She was not mourned publicly. Her "girls" were ordered to leave; the house would be sold to pay the county for her funeral expenses, and that was the end of the story. The Fergus Falls *Journal* was never as blunt in its own assessment as the Aitken Age, but it did see fit to reprint the short article.

The actors in this recent death tragedy at Fergus Falls, Lulu Harris and Nick Wilson, will be remembered quite well here, they having passed much of last winter at this village. … While Aitkin cannot claim them as bad citizens, yet our knowledge of what they were elsewhere leads us to feel that their absence leaves room in the world for better people. —Aitken Age reprinted in the Fergus Falls *Weekly Journal*, August 19, 1886.

12. A Drunken Rampage, March 1887

IN SELF-DEFENSE

WHILE SUFFERING FROM DELIRIUM TREMENS WOOD RUSHES THROUGH THE STREETS DEMOLISHING STORE FRONTS—HE PUTS SEVERAL CITIZENS TO FLIGHT BUT IS SHOT WHILE ATTACKING FRAZEE'S.

FULL ACCOUNT OF THE MANIAC'S DEEDS—NARROW ESCAPE OF PELICANITES—THE CORONER'S VERDICT.

Pelican Rapids, March 1 —Our usually quiet village has been thrown into a fever of excitement by the horrible tragedy which was enacted here early this morning. ... A good many naturally inquire why Lackey, Holmes and others did not follow the man when they knew he was in the streets ... the only blame that can be attached to any one is for not taking care of the man when he was known to be in such a condition. —Fergus Falls *Weekly Journal*, March 24, 1887

The "horrible tragedy" was the shooting of Arthur Wood by Theodore Frazee, a Pelican Rapids businessman. "Taking care of the man" was indeed what needed to be done. Wood's destruction of property was extensive, but the destructive forces raging inside him were at least as serious.

But Mr. Frazee should not carry the burden alone. Mr. Lackey was not only the proprietor of the hotel where the trouble brewed all night and into the next morning, he was also the town's constable. Arthur Wood's paranoia was at a peak, and he confronted both an ex-Marshall named Holmes, and Lackey. But rather than rally an ad hoc group to subdue Wood before anybody was hurt (including Wood himself), Lackey and Marshall both disappeared. The lone constable in town was not only absent, but he had also done nothing to alert the citizens of Pelican

Rapids, much less recruit some help to deal with the situation, and the "raving inebriate was permitted to get into the streets without any check and armed with his murderous bludgeon." But this, added, the Park Region *Pioneer*, its local newspaper, is what Pelicanites do.

... Pelicanites are very prone to decide that they are not their brother's keeper, and an excess of this feeling is perhaps at the root of that mysterious peculiarity in society here which so many notice but cannot define. —Park Region Pioneer, March 24, 1887.

Thomas Gillespie: Boyhood friends

When Arthur H. Wood came to Minnesota from Ohio, it was with the hope that he could brace up and stay away from drink. His friend and companion, Tom Gillespie, was only somewhat more in control, although not delusional. But with Wood's winter-long spree, even Gillespie could see that a change in Wood's environment was worth a try. So, Tom hauled him out to Lida Township in Otter Tail County, far away from Ohio, Wood's wife Jane and their four children.

Tom apologized to Jane when they left Ohio—at least he thought he did. The scene was muddled, and Tom was hazy on the sequence of events. Tom was sprawled on the woodpile by Wood's cabin. By some miracle, good ol' Artie was still standing, but he was waving a chunk of wood and hollering something about "those men!" at Tom.

"They here, Tom," he slurred. "C'mon! Geh-up!" and he rushed towards the cabin. But by that time, Jane was standing on the front step, her husband's double-barrel steadied on her shoulder and pointed right at his face.

"There, there! See?" Artie shouted, jabbing his finger in her direction.

"Get him outa here, Tom," she said, without lowering the gun. Artie may have been too wasted to comprehend the real danger, but it was plain enough to Tom. He'd talked Jane down a few times before, but this time he really didn't see the point. It was time to git.

The trip to Minnesota kept Tom on his toes and relatively sober, given the task of preventing Arthur from wandering off. Tom would lure him back in his seat by patting the bottle nestled in his jacket pocket. Artie slept a good piece, occasionally waking with a start to grab Tom's arm and urgently whisper, "Is that them? Back there, did they just get off? I saw 'em, Tom!"

"No, Artie, that wasn't them," Tom would answer. "I'm sure we lost them back in Chicago."

"You sure? They blowed up the tracks, ya know."

"Yep, I know, Artie, but that was back in West Virginia. We ain't anywhere near there now," Tom would tell him over and over.

Arthur Wood was just sixteen years old when he enlisted in the Union Army in the waning days of the War for Southern Independence. Sent to guard a rail line in West Virginia, boredom was the most constant enemy for the teenager, but it was also lonely, and it could be dangerous. They were in Confederate territory. The Union soldiers were sitting ducks for local boys, all rebels who could strike and vanish into the wooded hills like ghosts.

Artie woke up one night convinced that he was surrounded. A bullet whizzed by his head, and he instinctively returned the shot into the darkness. He hit something … someone, maybe, but was it a Reb or one of his own? He had no idea. The rebel strikes were intermittent, but enough to make sleep almost impossible. Boredom, short bursts of terror, then more boredom. The slugs of homemade whisky an older soldier shared with the boy were more than a welcome diversion.

R. E. Patterson: The Help of a Neighbor, March 14, 1887

Tom and Artie pulled into Pelican Rapids on a Monday night and put up in Lackey's hotel. The final trek to Tom's place at

Lida was not much over seven miles, but a hot meal and a whisky or two sounded more attractive than slogging through the half-froze mud in the damp wind of mid-March. They had more than a couple of whiskeys, though, and were still pretty well-lit when they headed out to Lida Tuesday morning with some basic provisions—and more whiskey.

By Wednesday night, Artie was beyond senseless. Tom, even in his inebriated state, knew Artie needed more help than Tom could provide, and at about 2:00 a.m. Thursday, Tom showed up with him at R.E. Patterson's place. Within two hours, Tom was lying spread-eagle on Patterson's bed in the corner, watching the rafters spin around him like the spokes on a wagon wheel. He dropped one foot to the floor to slow the rafters down, squinted through one eye, and tilted his head towards the fracas on the other side of the room. Wood was still wildly ranting about "the gang" and waving an open knife he'd snatched from Patterson's kitchen table. Tom was preoccupied with his left arm that was asleep. The rest of him was not far behind.

Patterson had to get Wood out of his house and into town. Maybe medical attention could handle this; Patterson certainly couldn't, especially on his own, Wood was a blacksmith by trade, and a stout man with powerful arms and shoulders. Patterson was no match and had to hope he could outsmart him, or there was little hope of anything but escape. Wood still refused to surrender the open knife in his hand, and Tom Gillespie lay passed out on the bed.

"I ain't goin' in no wagon!" Wood hollered. "The noise! The gang'll hear us, and they'll come for me!"

Patterson was able to convince him to *walk* into town, "so they could sneak past that gang," he told Wood. The trip was punctuated with stabs of the knife into the empty darkness, but eventually the threats turned to Patterson, who made up a diversion and by 5:00 a.m., Wood had given up his threats, and Patterson was pounding on Dr. Pattee's door in Pelican Rapids. Wood wouldn't take the medicine Dr. Pattee was quick to offer, though, so convinced was he that it was poison.

The next best remedy was food, so they headed to Lackey's Hotel for breakfast. The meal levelled him out enough to get him back to Dr. Pattee's for a dose of whatever the doc prescribed. At that point, Patterson would have shoved laudanum full-strength down Wood's throat to keep him on an even keel.

Whatever Pattee gave him, it worked well enough for Patterson to retrieve his knife and head back home. Wood passively roamed the streets for the rest of the day and took a room that night at Lackey's. All was well.

Until about 10:00 p.m.

...It is supposed that he got some whisky during the afternoon or evening, but about 10 o'clock he went to the dining room at Lackey's hotel and asked the girl to give him a butcher knife or ax, saying he wanted it to defend himself with during the night. Of course the girl did not give him the knife. —Fergus Falls *Weekly Journal*, March 24, 1887.

Early Morning, Friday, March 18

Lackey was grateful his serving girl had been smart about the knife, but he still worried about keeping Wood under his roof overnight. By 3:00 a.m., Lackey's concerns were realized with a loud crash from Wood's room, then hammering on the door with some kind of club. The guest next door, F.E. Holmes, checked to see what the trouble was. Wood charged from his room, brandishing the stick of birch wood, but Holmes scurried back to his room and locked the door.

Lackey appeared on the stairs and ordered Wood, in a useless interchange, to be quiet. Wood turned the attack on Lackey, pursued him down the stairs, and the chase was on. Lackey eluded him, once in the street, which sent Wood careening onward, across the bridge to the south end of Broadway, screaming "murder!" all the way. A.E. Rathburn was roused by the ruckus, with Wood hollering about three men that were killed at Lackey's, "and they're after me, too!" Wood's desperate escape charged ahead to the village's businesses: first A.G. Kinney's office, where he broke in the door; then Delong and Mickelson's Hardware, where several large panes of glass shattered under Wood's swinging club; the attack on the Post Office demolished its entire front window.

Splintered wood and shards of glass that sprayed across the wooden walkways marked Wood's path of destruction. It was mild for mid-March, but still no night to be out without proper clothing. The man, breathing hard, draped in nothing but a nightshirt, rivulets of his own blood from dozens of cuts streaming down his face, arms, and chest, paused and considered his next move. Dots of blood turned the melting snow pink by his bare feet. A breeze from the south tossed his hair across his face where it stuck.

Theodore Frazee's business was next. With renewed determination, Wood faced his next foe, demolishing Mr. Frazee's storefront—not just the glass, but all the sash, too. In his dwelling above the store, Theodore Frazee pulled on his trousers, thumbed his suspenders over his nightshirt, grabbed a gun and hurried down the stairs, where he met Wood, waving a large stick of wood. Wood lunged at this latest threat, but the heavy stick swung wide, time enough for Frazee to get off three shots, as Wood advanced again. Frazee wasn't taking any chances and left to reload, but when he returned, Wood was lying in the street, a bloody mess of ghastly cuts, none of them lethal. It was a single bullet wound that felled him. He was taken to lockup, where everything was done that could be done, but by mid-morning, he was dead.

Coroner Bedford came up from Fergus, and impannelled (sic) a jury ... The testimony of witnesses went to show that the man's insanity was caused by whisky ... The jury brought in a verdict as follows: "We, the jury, find that Arthur H. Wood came to his death by a bullet wound at the hands of Theo. Frazee; that the same was fired in defense of himself and property; and, further, we fully exonerate him from any responsibility." ... Many are asking what will be done with Mr. Frazee and whether or not the coroner's verdict is final. It is not and anyone who is desirous to do so can cause Mr. Frazee's arrest, but it is not thought that anyone will do so as it is so plain a case of self-defense. —Fergus Falls *Weekly Journal*, March 24, 1887.

This time, it was the killer who was sober and completely within his rights to shoot a man armed with a stick of wood—a man plagued with uncontrolled drinking, suffering from paranoid delusions and incapable of managing something as simple as getting a meal or going to bed. It was this man who was considered so dire a threat that it was acceptable to fire three shots at him to stop him from breaking more store windows.

Frazee, one might argue, overreacted. But as in the case of J.W. Sanders shooting a drunken Ed Brunson 13 years previously, law enforcement was not available—or didn't show up—to defend them and protect their property, much less assess the danger of the situation.

In the 1880s, it was often impossible to contact law enforcement in time to get help in a crisis situation. That's not necessarily true today, but similar arguments about handling addiction crises persist. The hometown newspaper wasn't holding back about its stance. The Fergus Falls paper took an approach more likely to find sympathetic readers today.

In an anxiety to make it appear that this village of our love is a perfectly safe and beatific place of residence, some may go too far in the suppression of truth. Nothing can be gained by it; everybody knows that a town having three establishments licensed to sell as a beverage the "stuff that steals away men's reason" cannot enjoy absolute immunity from brawls and panics. It is enough to exult over what 1st-of-May promises to bring, and over the glorious two -thirds vote by which our adult male folk have expressed their determination to abolish the riot-breeding element here. —*Park Region Pioneer*, March 24, 1887.

The only blame that can be attached to any one is for not taking care of the man when he was known to be in such a condition. —Fergus Falls *Weekly Journal,* March 24, 1887.

Part 2. FRONTIER JUSTICE

The photograph shows a girl with hair parted in the middle and pulled up in a knot low on her neck, according to the style of the day. She had large, dark eyes, and the full, round face of a young teen. As she aged, her face may have settled into the defined cheekbones and chiseled features of a real beauty. In the vernacular of the day, she might have been considered quite "a catch," certainly not a proper match for an odd Norwegian man twice her age, described as "diminutive," of limited intellectual ability, and unremarkable but for his peculiarities. But there's no evidence that anyone who knew him anticipated a capacity for violence.

Unless it was Lillie herself.

Reports about the crime strongly suggest she was afraid of him, but why? Had he tried something with her before? Why did she think he was "a bad man," as Nels Holong, her killer, related? What did she know that others did not, or they knew and didn't take seriously? She must have complained to someone.

Lillie's story *is* haunting, but not because Lillie's specter is floating around the old farmstead. What hangs on is its eerie familiarity: a girl alone with a man is killed. Our inability still today to bring an end to this tragedy is a dark splotch that never fades, no matter how much time passes.

Lillie may not have feared for her life, but she certainly didn't feel safe, and that should have been enough. Once her little brother left to return a shovel to the neighbors, there was almost no chance that the man's advances, if that's what he had in mind, would be discovered. She did the only thing she had available to her to try and scare him off. She grabbed a knife. No one, including a 15-year-old girl in 1887, pulls a knife on a man unless she feels desperate. Nels Holong may have seemed innocuous to everyone else, but he was a very real threat *to her*.

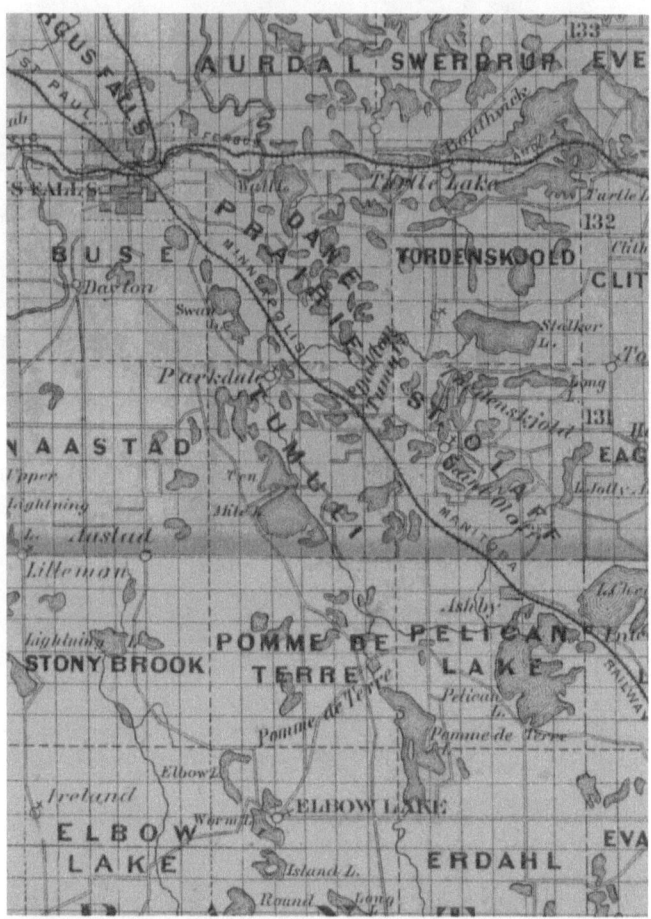

5. From the 1884 "Outline Plan of Otter Tail County, Minnesota" showing Fergus Falls south to St. Olaf township, and part of Grant County where the Field's Pomme de Terre farm was located. Nels Holong walked from the Field's farm in the northern part of St. Olaf to Pomme de Terre, and on to Wendell, just north and west of Elbow Lake, the next day. Map provided by the Otter Tail County Historical Society Museum.

1. The Fields: A Home in St. Olaf

C harles Field, Lillie's older brother, sent a handwritten note to E.F. Barnard, Secretary of the Otter Tail County Historical Society, in January 1930, Charles was a resident of the State Hospital in Fergus Falls at the time.

Father A.W. Field took his squatters claim in what is now St. Olaf (The land was not surveyed by the government at that time) What is now sec 3+2. south of Fields or Song Lake in the fall of 1867. ... He was a soldier at Old Pomme De Terre before that and picked out his claim when he was a soldier at the stockade. He moved from Filmore County. With Ox Teams. In the fall of 1868 Father Went down to Pewaukee (17 miles west of Milwaukee on what was the Milwaukee & Water Town Plank Road) & brought out Mother and us three children in Feb. 1869 ... We still have the old farm in St. Olaf.

Yours Truly, C.B. Field.

P.S. I was born in Aug 1857 before the Civil War.

Charles, Lillie's Big Brother, 1868–1869

Mother was distraught when Father finally joined up. He'd been shrewd about enlisting, but with good reason. Esther was born the year the War broke out, and I was too little to be much help. He might have left in '63 if little Perry hadn't come along then.

With the tide turning in the summer of 1864, Father could avoid the inevitable no more, and signed up, serving with Company D, 3rd Wisconsin Infantry. He missed Antietam and Gettysburg and, oddly, felt slighted, as if he should have lent his name to what quickly became famous battles. He never spoke of his one major battle: Bentonville, North Carolina. I heard it from other soldiers, who returned to their farms and businesses in the summer of '65 with the end of the War.

Father was driven to make a name for himself … somehow … and he couldn't get out of Wisconsin fast enough. "It's over here," he'd say. I didn't know what was over—I was only seven or eight at the time—but if Father said it, I believed it. All he could talk about was "free land" and "a new start." Mother alternated between lashing out at him and retreating into exhausted silence. I was old enough to help Father with feeding the stock and other farm chores by then. Esther wasn't much help in the house yet, but Father took special interest in his beautiful little girl. Perry was always getting into things; Father had no time for "the little hellion," as he called him.

His spare moments were spent reading about "squatters claims" and "opportunity." While others planned to head for the vast Western plains or the hills of California beyond that, Father had narrowed his search to Minnesota. Much easier to get to, and he'd be one of the first, he'd say. A farmer who thought like a businessman could make a killing.

By the time Father left to take up a new post at the Pomme de Terre stockade in Minnesota, Mother was glad to see him go. She didn't have to deal with his obsession about free land every waking moment. He wrote in August of 1867 that he'd taken his squatter's claim near Pomme de Terre in a place called St. Olaf. Late in February of '69, our family saw St. Olaf.

It was a small cabin near a pond sheltered by huge hardwoods, their branches just bare sticks, this time of year, waving aimlessly in the wind off the prairie. Mother saw only more hard work, following after "Father's nonsense," as she called it. It made him all the more determined to be right about moving there. He had already turned over a corner of a nearby meadow and planted potatoes, he said, but all we saw was snow. Everywhere there was snow, drifting as high as the top of the wagon wheels. We had one cow, and Father was immensely proud of the rooster and two hens that he had nesting in one end of the cowshed he'd put up.

"Fresh eggs and milk!" he'd bellow.

"We had that in Wisconsin!" she'd holler right back.

Esther and Lillie, June 23, 1878

She looked out the window June 23, 1878, and saw blue sky. Esther untied the braid in her dark brown hair, shook the waves out and let them tumble down her back. The air was thick with dragonflies—late this year, so one species battled another for the morning's hatch of mosquitoes and midges. Their aerobatics distracted her for a moment until she glanced back into the room, shared with her little sister Lillie, still asleep, and saw the sun splashing across her wedding costume, hanging on the hook behind the door: a deep, creamy satin bodice with oodles of covered buttons, a skirt bedecked with a fine bustle of the same delicious fabric, and a bonnet fringed with lace from her mother's wedding suit. If her mother had had her way, the whole wedding suit would have been reworked for this day.

"Just as well," her mother sniffed. "Why spend needlessly on a color she'll never wear again!"

But Father wouldn't hear of it. His oldest daughter was marrying a young farmer from Grant County—practically a neighbor—from a family that was prospering in their labors.

"She'll have her own dress, by God!" he announced. "And that's final!"

Esther assured her mother that she'd make the costume herself—Mrs. Risbrudt was nearby and could help if Mother was too busy. "Really, Mother, I'm sure we'll manage. You have so many things to think about," Esther told her, enormously grateful that she didn't have to rebuild a moldy old suit from before The Rebellion in the South—or offend her mother with the disappointment Esther couldn't have concealed.

So, there it was, shimmering, it seemed to Esther, in the morning sun of this fine June day. Her father even paid for a proper corset made in Minneapolis that turned Esther's strong body into a perfect hourglass shape. She felt ravishing in it! Wilford Burns would be speechless when he saw her walk down the aisle on her father's arm. But Will *never* talked much, she thought, and giggled about the last time he had kissed her with not so much as a pretty word at first. But his smile and soft eyes said everything. If he had stripped her cotton dress off her right there, she wouldn't have stopped him, and she was sure he felt just the same. Her father's call had sent her back to their wagon in the Burns' yard, but Father had most certainly noticed the mist sparkling in her eyes.

Father just smirked, raised one eyebrow, and said, "Get in, girl. I see it's time to get you home."

She giggled, flung herself up on the wagon seat and turned her face to the sun drifting lower on the horizon. Will was hers; she was so proud of this fact. In a few weeks she'd be in his arms every night. The thrill of it had made her shiver, which made her father look at her and cock his eyebrow again.

It made her shiver now, and she tossed a shawl over her shoulders and glanced at Lillie. "She'll be a pretty girl one day, when she grows out of her baby fat," she thought, "and if she'd just smile." Esther dashed to the kitchen in her bare feet. Mother had made coffee, which smelled heavenly, and she couldn't wait to have some.

Esther's Baby, August 10, 1880

The back bedroom in the split log home was already stifling at nine o'clock in the morning. Instead of clearing the air and bringing relief to the laboring woman in the bed, the thunderstorm that rolled through Grant County had just added to the humidity of this hot and still August day, and Esther's pain dragged on.

"My feet don't hurt," Esther told Lillie. "I'll think about my feet." And then another wave of pain would pour itself out from inside of her and grip her with such intensity that she barely knew where her feet were, and she couldn't breathe at all.

Her mother-in-law dabbed at her face with a wet cloth and let the young woman pinch her hands with the new pains that clutched at her womb with terrifying ferocity and engulfed her from her neck to ankles. Esther had wanted to swat the stupid rag away and scream at the older woman to do something useful and stop the pain, but hours of this had stolen any energy left to protest.

Her mother-in-law had abandoned the soft, friendly expression she'd adopted for this ordeal in order to reassure her daughter-in-law that all this would pass, and a lovely baby would be born. Now, her forehead wrinkled, she wrapped her lips tightly over her teeth and took frequent looks out the window. Esther's mother, Priscilla, took the seat by the bed and set down a basin of fresh, colder water on the bedside table. Lillie had followed her in, barely daring to glance at her sister. By now Esther's skin was hot and weirdly dry to the touch.

"Where is that Doctor!" Priscilla snapped at her, and the baby inside her kicked out, but just once. Priscilla had all but forgotten while Esther labored that her own baby was due in little more than a month. They would be close in every way she had imagined, but an escalating panic was building inside her.

"Sent for, Mama. I'll go see," Lillie answered, and dashed from the room, dragging Roselie, Esther's sister-in-law, with her. Roselie was only too happy to escape the torment of watching Esther—just one year older than herself! Struggling to survive at all, by this point. It had been hours and hours— since yesterday sometime. But then it was happy anticipation. Excitement! A new baby in the house, and she would be an auntie. Her older brother, Will, was swaggering around the kitchen like he was the first man to ever father a child.

"Get out of here, now!" Roselie's mother had said, swatting his shoulder with a dish towel, but she was snickering. "Get us some fresh water—and lots of it." That was yesterday. "Leave us be," she whispered with purpose. "This is going to take a while."

But nobody thought it would take this long.

Another cry from the bedroom, deep and throaty, stopped them both at the door. It was followed by a gasp and then nothing. Lillie started running down the Burns' road. She couldn't stay there in that room; she just couldn't. She would run until she found the doctor, drag him from his buggy, and make him run to the house with her. She would! "Don't die, Esther, please don't die!" she said over and over, as if the worst could not happen as long as she kept saying it. "Don't die, don't die, don't die!"

The doctor showed up, sure enough, and somehow saved the baby, but not for long, and Esther was gone. Ragnil Pederson, who was feeding her own twins, offered to nurse the poor little thing. But the scrawny boy could barely suck, and when he did, it was not nearly long enough to get the food he needed. Mrs. Pederson all but lived at their house with her babies, Joey and Rudolph, and the extended family cheered themselves with imagining the three boys growing up together and getting into all sorts of mischief one day. But it was fruitless to hope such things; in little more than a week Harry H. Burns was laid to rest next to his mother.

Lillie sobbed for days until her mother could endure no more and sent her to weed the garden, disregarded while they had been fussing over the baby. Fussing wasn't helping, but none of them would leave him to do anything else, and the weeds had completely hidden the green beans, cucumbers and beets. Lillie would be kept busy, and she could howl all she wanted out there.

Lillie growled and grunted as she tugged violently at the crab grass and quack grass, flinging it to the ends of the rows. When every single shred of a weed had been cleared around a bean plant, she dug her fingers into the soil, and dug and dug, all along the bean row, until she reached earth that was still damp and cool. Then she lay down in it, stared up at the clouds gathering to the southwest, vowed she would never marry, and stopped crying.

Charles: Another Little Brother! September 29, 1880

And what a rascal his little brother turned out to be! It's a good thing Lillie was around to help out because that little guy was worse than Perry. Mother hadn't expected to have another baby at her age and was plagued by a jumble of emotions, what with Esther and her baby gone. Beautiful Esther and her fragile little boy … gone! Every time she looked at her own squawking baby in the cradle, she was tormented by guilt and would collapse in bewilderment. How could things happen this way? It was too much, but time to mourn would have been a luxury. As Clark grew and took to exploring the farm on his own, Mother just gave up on raising him. As long as he didn't wreck anything or seriously hurt himself, Clark did what he liked. Scratches and scrapes—and there were many—were ignored. He had to be screaming his head off or bleeding good to get her attention. I never saw such a tough little kid.

There was more to it, I suppose. Hard to tell because Mother didn't say much. Losing Esther and her baby made a different person out of her. She rarely looked right at me—or anybody—and never started a conversation, not even to ask for help when she unloaded the wagon, unless she was getting after Lillie. She just lived by herself, no matter how many people were in the house.

That didn't make it any easier for Lillie, who was about eleven then. She got stuck with her little brother a lot, and she had little interest. All she wanted was to be with her friends and go to school. If Mother just would've talked to her, they might not have been at each other so much when Lillie was home.

Father, however, got a big kick out of Clark, but the kid was like a puppy that one kicked to the side once it got too annoying. Mother finally got her way with a name, though. She'd always told me that, as the oldest, I should have had her maiden name, "Clark." That was the proper way to do it, but Father didn't go for that. Here this little guy, born in a land new and wild—where Mother never wanted to be—grew up just as wild. It turned out the way it should be. Clark belonged here, more than any of us. Lilly, too. She never knew another home, either.

Under the Waves, November 25, 1884

Last week Tuesday was an unlucky day for A.W. Fields of St. Olaf. As himself and son were returning from Herman, where they had been to dispose of two load of grain, Mr. Fields, who was driving the lightest of his two teams, in order to save distance, drove upon the lake near Cowing's store. —Fergus Falls *Weekly Journal*, December 2, 1884.

Alphonso Field was sure of himself. When he said something, he meant it, and he wouldn't back down. So, when he told Charles to follow him across the lake by Cowing's Store, Charles followed, even though he was out of his teens and old enough to question his father's wisdom in doing so. It had been a mild winter so far, with enough early snow to insulate what little ice there was. None of the deep, definitive temperatures of previous winters had yet materialized—the kind of weather that could make inches of ice overnight with ice that boomed and belched to announce its formation.

His son, who was driving the heavy team, followed his father on to the ice, which gave no signs of weakness when the light team passed over it.

Alphonso, with the lighter team, had tossed the smaller load of family provisions in Charles' wagon, pulled by their Belgians. Their load of grain safely delivered in Herman, it was just a matter of getting home to St. Olaf, or at least as far as their farm in Pomme de Terre, Grant County, which was closer.

But it was late afternoon, and even in early December a pall settled in by about four o'clock on an overcast day. Alphonso was determined to cross the lake and save a few miles. The day had been pleasant enough, but deep purple clouds to the northwest signaled a change was likely. In seconds he had

126

guided his team down the easy embankment and the pair was trotting across the wide bay.

Charles' team balked at the shoreline and pawed the sand, dancing side to side with their front hooves. He slapped the reins harder and called "Hyah!" until the team started out on the frozen surface. Alonzo was far ahead by this time; his little bays had tripped over the ice with ease, but it was cracking under Charles' heavier team, sending long faults shooting across the graying ice.

The boy says that for quite a little distance, the ice cracked beneath the weight of his team and water appeared upon the surface, but he supposed it strong enough, as his father had just passed safely over it.

By the time one the ice opened under the team, Charles was too far from shore to turn back, and the team broke through with a giant heave of ice chunks and lake water. He leaped from the wagon and flung himself towards the closest unbroken surface, catching the edge of firmer ice just as the wagon pulled the team under, the momentum carrying them beneath the solid ice beyond, and they were gone.

The horses screams and the sound of ice pitching skyward finally reached his father's ears and Alphonso made for shore to follow it back as close as he could get to Charles, who was submerged up to his neck and clinging to the fractured edge of the ice, gasping with the cold.

"Climb up on the ice, boy!" his father shouted. "Get on there now!"

Buoyed by his father's calls, he heaved himself onto the ice and walked towards shore to meet him. By this time, Mr. Hammer, who lived nearby and had seen the event, raced to offer what help he could. Hammer thought Alphonso took the loss coolly and was going to wrap Charles in a blanket and keep going. But Hammer wouldn't have it, and brought them to his house for dry clothes, at least, before he sent them on his way.

"This loss, Mr. Field ..." Hammer said, while Charles shed his wet clothes in the corner of the cabin. "That looked to be a valuable team you had," he added.

"Oh, yes, that it was," Field said, and turned to Charles. "Get a move on! We're still a long ways from home, boy." And he strode to the wagon, his wool jacket flapping open in the wind rising up from the northwest.

Charles sprinted after his father, who with reins in hand, was mounting the seat.

"Father, the horses ..." Charles asked, dropping on the wagon seat.

"We'll come back some warmer day and fish them out," he answered and slapped the reins over the team's backs.

What would mother say? In fact, what would Charles tell her? She wouldn't believe Father's version—he was quite sure of that—so he would have to say something. He knew what he wanted to say. *Father is crazy, Mother! You know that!* But there was no need. The darkness that settled in her eyes, her lips curled over her teeth, her shoulders stiff as she turned her back on him ... he knew she knew it, too. He would reassure her as best he could.

"Thank you, Mr. Hammer!" Charles called back to him, grabbing at the corners of the blanket to wrap around his shoulders. "I'll return the clothes!"

... This loss falls heavily upon Mr. Field, as the team was a valuable one worth fully $500. —Fergus Falls *Weekly Journal,* December 2, 1884.

Priscilla Field: Unbelievable, September 13, 1886

Clark was only five, but he could already open the gate to let the cows in to milk, and he wasn't the least bit afraid of the hens pecking at him when he picked eggs. He'd stuff his hand right under a sitting hen and grab the eggs so quick that he had them in the basket before the hen knew what to peck at. Priscilla Field couldn't remember her youngest ever being afraid—of anything. As soon as he knew how to lift the latch on the kitchen door, there was no keeping him inside, and off he went.

Since he'd filled the wood bin like she told him to, she let him go when she heard the latch again that morning. He was off to the barn, jumping off the beams in the hayloft most likely. This time of year, there was plenty of hay, right up to the beams in some places. Might as well just let him burn off some energy, so she could get some morning chores done without him underfoot.

She was thinking about Clark and wondering how she'd keep such a boy alive long enough to grow up, when she decided to go see if he'd make it until lunch, at least. She slipped on the clogs outside by the door—they hurt her bunions, but she wasn't about to track in all that straw and whatnot—pulled her bonnet tight over her ears and headed across the yard.

When she slid open the barn door, the late September's stiff breeze kicked up the loose straw in the opening, and the rush of dusty air banged the door against the wall. She heard it before she saw anything and knew the sound even though she'd never heard it before—not like that. The "squeak squeak … squeak squeak" of the rope as he swung back and forth, dangling like a pull toy from the center beam between the stalls. Clark turned around and looked at her. "Who has Father's clothes on?" was all he said.

She grabbed his arm with one hand, her skirts with the other, and half-dragged him over the dry leaves mounded randomly across the yard, like dirt piled on a fresh grave. The wind was gusting pretty good, but all she could hear was that damn squeaking!

She bent down close to his flushed little face and barked, "Get over to Olson's and get Torger. Quick! Before he's back in the field after dinner!" Her shaking voice rattled the boy, and he took off running to the Field's nearest neighbor.

Rage was swallowing her whole. She needed her sons. She needed her Esther, too, but Esther was dead. Clark was a boy in miniature by now, arms flailing like a marionette as he scampered over the furrows in the field between the two homesteads. Worthless sobs finally escaped her in gasps and howls. "Everybody dies!" She screamed in the direction of the barn, but there was no one to hear her.

He was so handsome! So incredibly handsome! ... No. Her husband was beautiful. Loads of dark hair curled in soft waves around his head with ordered perfection. His mouth was framed by an equally perfect dark moustache, sparkling with bits of silver, the first indication of his advancing age. But his eyes! Large, almost black and fringed with lashes so thick that he was forever pulling on them. It all would have been too much on a lesser man, but he wore it with casual disinterest, which only added to his appeal for her. Unbelievably beautiful.

Everything about him, in fact, was just a little unbelievable. When it wasn't unsettling, or downright disrupting, it was tantalizingly unbelievable. Life with a man whose mental hinges were loose and jangling from rusting chains ... one always wondered about when it could happen, and a link could break free. The noise in the man's head must have been deafening at times. Who knows what he was suffering? Did he know how he teetered on the edge of life, jerking her precariously with him? Life was so ... so *big* with him—too big for everybody else around him, though they all tried to embrace it. Well, the children knew nothing else.

Lillie especially adored him. Thank God she was still at school! What was Priscilla going to say to her? Just fourteen and the apple of her father's eye. He let her do whatever she wanted, and the girl chafed under her mother's attempts to discipline her. Even with Alphonso alive, there was a battle brewing with that one.

"Oh, my God! Now what?" Priscilla gasped, and then a scream escaped, and then another. When she couldn't scream anymore, she ran to the grove and wretched until there was nothing left to come out of her. She was walking back to the house when Torger showed up with Ole, his oldest boy.

"I left Clark with Kjerste," he said. "What's happened, Priscilla?"

2. Nels Holong Leaves Home

Otter Tail County is big, sort of square, and holds down a mostly west central spot in the state. At 2,225 square miles, it is an unwieldy size—a piece easily found and placed, if Minnesota counties were a jigsaw puzzle. Seemingly endless hardwood forests, pristine lakes and streams, and so much rich soil that had never been planted, it was full of promise for people like Alphonso Field.

A good farm worker had a chance here, and Nils Hålång (Americanized to Nels Holong) must have felt lucky when Alphonso Field hired him. Nels left his family's farm in Winneshiek County, Iowa, sometime in 1882, his descendants believe. His parents, Ragnild Petersdatter and Ole Holong, were Norwegian immigrants and founders of Madison Lutheran Church near Decorah. The "baby of the family," Nels was confirmed there, probably in 1870, at fifteen years old. A confirmand was an adult in the eyes of the church and free to make his own way in the world, to take over a man's job either at home, or to hire out. But it was a good ten years before Nels left home.

He eventually found the Red River Valley, west and north of the Field's homestead, but by 1886, he had landed in Otter Tail County. Alphonso Field was expanding his operation with his son Charles taking a farm in adjacent Grant County. He hired Holong to work for Charles, who was pleased with his work and decided to keep him on through the winter and the farming season: seven months for 150 dollars. Nels had a new home, work that he understood and reliable wages. He also had an interest in Charles' younger sister, Lillie.

Ingeborg Holong Helle, Spring, 1881

Nels finally left home when he was twenty-five. Nels's oldest sister, Ingeborg, said, "finally" not because she wanted him to go, but because most men were married or betrothed at that age. Ingeborg and her husband Ole married and had five children. They lost four of them. Then she buried Ole, too.

Nels had never even had a sweetheart. Ingeborg suspected that no one would have him, and their parents thought he would finally grow up if he had to be out on his own. But it was disturbing for Ingeborg, because one day he was there, and the next he was gone.

Every morning he had appeared at Mother's table, waiting for her to put a mug of tea and slices of bread in front of him. She was not married to this man. Another woman should now be putting his tea and bread in front of him! That's what her siblings thought but never said in front of Nels or their parents. Since Ingeborg was the oldest, the siblings confided in her—even Mother. She scrubbed his clothes and admonished him to scrape his boots and leave them at the door. He wasn't a child. She shouldn't have to say anything anymore. She'd say this under her breath just to Ingeborg. "Couldn't he just remember?" she'd add, but she was staring past Ingeborg, and the daughter couldn't bear to answer. He could remember. It just didn't matter enough.

When Mother casually mentioned the names of some of the single girls in their church, Nels just looked at her with pale, empty blue eyes, as if he was trying to process what all that might mean to him … *If he were to talk to one of them, what would she think? Would he have to take her home, then? What would happen next?* … It was too much to think about. He would go back to slurping his tea. She would go back to telling him not to slurp.

Ingeborg didn't know what finally prompted him to leave the house. Father's mouth would close tightly, and his brow would wrinkle. He wouldn't answer and she knew better than to press the issue. Surely Father would miss Nels's help around the farm. They had done well, and that meant more animals to care for, more grain and hay to harvest, more fences to repair—more of everything. Mother must have convinced herself that Nels knew what he needed to sustain himself. He was a decent farm hand. That might be enough.

He knew right from wrong, too; Father was a strong disciplinarian. Nels couldn't quite make it through Luther's Catechism, but he knew the Lord's Prayer well enough and as much as he'd fidget in church—absentmindedly scratching along his hairline, where his cap usually sat; drumming his fingers on his knee; staring out the little window as he sat at the end of the pew—he never complained about attending. But what did he actually hear, much less absorb out of their careful instruction in Lutheran theology and the teachings of Our Lord? Mother worried for his soul. Ingeborg overheard her telling Father this. He revealed little of what might have plagued his heart about his youngest son. That was fine for women, but he was certainly above it.

Ingeborg couldn't have imagined setting out alone like that and leaving their family so far behind. But America (all of it, I suppose) was home to him, having been born here. He didn't know the family's real home, as his older siblings and parents did. He was comfortable in that, and it comforted Ingeborg when he came and said goodbye to her. He said he knew there was work on the farms in Southern Minnesota that were getting bigger than anything in Iowa. He would smile—even laugh—but there were so few details, that she knew he had no more understanding of where he was going than her big shepherd dog that thumped his tail while Nels scratched his ears. She fought back tears and clung to him one last time. "*Lille broren min!*" she told him and forced a little laugh. He would always be her little brother.

The Pomme de Terre Farm, Grant County, March 1887

In the half-light of the approaching evening, the hunched figure walking with measured, deliberate steps toward the little house appeared imposing enough to elicit a low growl from the dog, with front feet planted in a melting snowbank, and back feet breaking through an icy mud puddle. It was a transitional time of year, the seasons demanded change, and change was sometimes good.

The figure—his name was Nels—was short enough to be an adolescent, but thick enough to be an adult. He paused when the dog let out a sharp warning bark. He was upwind. "Magnus! Komme!" he called, and the dog came running, hackles down and ears up, bounding through the icy mix of snow, mud and last year's buffalo grass.

"Figured he'd show up sooner or later," Nels thought. "Ladwig's bitch must be in heat," and the little collie dog bounced against his leg and gaily grabbed his coat sleeve all the way back to the little house. "That's the way I'd feel, too," he told the dog, "if I had a roll in the hay with my gal." But he'd just lost another lamb, and that wasn't good at all.

The split logs of the house had already grayed out; they shimmered in the half-moon's light. Nels grabbed an armload of split wood stacked by the door and stepped inside. Magnus thumped his tail, anticipating a warm spot to stretch out when Nels got the fire going.

Nels lit the lamp on the table by the cookstove and set it by the wash basin. When Charles hired him for this job at the Field family's Pomme de Terre farm, Lillie had said to him, "You take good care of Father's sheep," so she would ask about them. He'd lost two lambs already, and he would have to tell her. He scrubbed his hands with the lye soap resting in a tin bowl. With 160 head, some ewes were going to drop their lambs early and they'd not make it. But that argument wouldn't get anywhere with her, he said to the face in the small mirror nailed on the wall above the wash basin.

He lingered over that face ... long, reddish brown scraps of a beard that crawled right up to his cheekbones and down his neck. His hair had grown long, with thick, disorderly shocks cupping his ears and standing up on the top of his head, trained into a pattern set by his habit of pulling his cap on from the back and tugging the ear flaps over whatever landed inside them.

Lillie wasn't quite his gal, but she would be someday, he thought. She'd said something about getting a picture took, and that was just like an engagement, wasn't it?

He pulled a jack knife out of his pocket, and without bothering to rinse off the remainder of the lamb's placenta stuck to it, he took after the first bunch of hair he grabbed. Then another and another, until it was short enough all over to wash in the basin and lay down flat under his cap.

Next would be a shave—his first in weeks—and a trim of his thick moustache. He took great care with it, in order to look like the well-off men who ran businesses in town. Even Brandenburg, the sheriff in Otter Tail County, had a moustache like this.

He took out his Sunday coat—a hand-me-down from his older brother—scrubbed the collar and cuffs in the only clean snow left near the house, brushed it carefully and hung it from the rafter above the woodstove to get it aired out and dry. It had been a long time since he had gone to church. Grue Lutheran wasn't far, and it was Norwegian, so he'd know what was going on, but he wasn't sure he could remember all the service.

His father would be disappointed in him about that. He knew he was expected to go to church every Sunday. He wondered what his father would think of Lillie Field. If they got married, it would most likely take place at Grue Lutheran Church. From what he could tell, the Fields didn't have a church. Anyway, he hadn't been to church since he'd moved in last fall to the house that Lillie's older brother, Charles, had provided. Maybe it had been longer than that.

He had seen Lillie only a few times during last fall's threshing, and he couldn't be sure that he would see her when he visited his Norwegian friends near the Field's home place, but he thought he might, and he should be ready. It would be nice to talk Norwegian with his friends and not have to work so hard and figure out what people were saying in English. He would teach Lillie Norwegian. That thought made him smile.

3. The Man Who Loved Lillie Field, May 26, 1887

T he door banged open. Charles didn't see anyone in the kitchen yet and hollered, "Let's get a move on!" He paused, thinking of the full day they had planned in Fergus Falls, eighteen miles away. "Mother! We have a lot to do!" Five-year-old Clark raced past him with a chunk of bread in his little fist.

"Where's Mr. Holong?" Lillie called from upstairs.

"Hitching the team. Get down here!"

"Quit ordering me around!" she screamed back at him.

That girl had a mouth on her, that's for sure. It irked Charles to no end, and frankly, he didn't have much interest in being a dad to her, but he had no choice. Somebody had to take over for Father, and it wasn't going to be Mother.

Last night there'd been another row that had become routine between Mother and Lillie. "No, you are not going to school and you're not going into town!" Mother had shouted as she piled supper scraps in a bowl for the pigs. "You are going to get the laundry done, take care of your little brother and get Mr. Holong's dinner, and there is no more to say about it." Her mother always called him "Mr. Holong." She didn't care to be too familiar with hired help.

"But Mrs. Risbrudt can't come over and neither can Christi."

Then Charles chimed in. "You can't handle a few chores by yourself? Some girls your age go hire out in town, you know."

"My friends will be in school tomorrow, you know!" she fired back at her brother.

"One day of chores. That's all! You're so damn smart, I see no reason why you can't miss a day of school," he answered in a calmer voice. He wanted to keep this from getting out of hand—again.

"It's not that!" But Lillie was already a mess of tears. "I'm not staying here with that Mr. Holong!"

He'd seen Nels—Mr. Holong—looking at her, but it seemed to him that there was no harm in Nels doing so. Charles found it funny that it bothered Lillie. Nels was just so … different. There was no way a smart, spunky girl like Lillie was going to take an interest in that odd little Norwegian. He had to be fifteen years older anyway. Not that he'd ever want Lillie to marry somebody like that. The thought of it made him snort.

"What are you laughing at?" Lillie demanded, wiping her damp face with her apron.

"Nothing." But Charles couldn't help himself and let go of a good guffaw.

Lillie gave an exasperated growl that she'd perfected since she became a teenager and piled up the supper dishes with an unusual amount of clattering. "Grrrr!"

"What's the matter? Don't want to give him that picture you got took of you?"

"You shut up about that picture!"

"And you be careful how you speak to me, Miss."

"I never promised him no picture. I said he could maybe see them. He's so stupid! He just didn't even know what I said!" and Lillie whirled away and stomped up the stairs.

Charles hadn't seen her since that episode after supper, but with her frequent outbursts he thought little more about it until the next morning when Lillie bolted from the kitchen, pulling her apron off with one hand and holding her straw bonnet in the other. "Mama, please. Can't we go with you?"

"I don't want Clark underfoot, and who do you suppose is going to get the laundry done?"

"I'll get it done!" Lillie hollered.

"When?"

Lillie didn't answer. Her eyes landed on Mr. Holong, who was just standing—doing nothing—by the pasture gate. Watching the house. Or her. Then the sun edged over the hill and blinded her, blocking out that annoying picture.

"All right. When you're done, you can drop Clark at Olson's and go off with your friends. But leave some supper for Mr.

Holong," Mother said and climbed up on the wagon seat. "He'll probably be happy to not have to look at you mooning around like a sick heifer."

Charles clucked to the horses and the wagon jolted forward. Mother turned back to her and called, "I told Clark you'd catch frogs with him later!" Charles clucked again and the team broke into a trot.

"Mother! He feeds them to snakes!" she hollered back.

Charles had to laugh; he just couldn't help it.

Lillie broke into a run, following the wagon's dust. "Don't leave me here! Don't leave me!" she screamed. "Please don't leave me!"

Nels, Later That Morning

The bright spring green of late April had deepened into the richer, darker color of late May. The woods, sloughs and meadows grew thick with vegetation and teamed with tiny black flies and the first hatch of mosquitoes. With the wheat grass up to their bellies in places, it was the time of year when horses could founder if you let them out in the pasture too long. Nels knew how to look for the stripes on their hooves that signaled trouble.

In fact, farm chores were something he understood, and the day started out all right. He did the milking and let the cows out to graze. But he left the gate open to the pasture and just when he got to the barn, he had to walk back and latch it. He also forgot to put the lid on the milk can and the cats were yowling and scratching over it to get their share. He chased them off, slammed down the lid, and thought what to do about his stomach that was flipping over and over.

He wanted some tea, but Lillie would be in the kitchen doing the laundry, and as much as he wanted to be with her, he didn't want her to see him like this with a flushed face and his hands shaking. She was so pretty, and he had thought of nothing else since he came to help out here at the Field's home place in St. Olaf, where she lived. He didn't like that she did this to him, but he couldn't seem to help himself, either, so he grabbed at tufts of his reddish brown hair, and tugged at the corners of his moustache by way of making himself more presentable, and at last, he went to the house—his hands deep in his pockets, fingering his pocket knife for something to do, and softly singing a little song his mother had taught him ... *"Per Spelemann, han hadde ei einaste ku ..."* The Fields might have just one cow, too, just like Per Spelemann, if Nels forgot to latch the gate again.

He kicked at some weeds that had sprouted in the path to the house. Just something to do, while he thought about how he would talk to her now that they would be alone all day and well into the evening. He'd only been to Fergus Falls once, but he knew it was far. Clark might be around, but that little kid didn't stay in one place for long, and he sure didn't pay attention to adults much, so Nels didn't worry about Clark.

But Lillie ... he worried over her. Her dark eyes and thick lips gave her an imposing look, and she didn't smile. Still, he loved the little curls that fell from her tightly wound bun and stuck to her neck when she sweated as she cleared the dinner dishes. She was almost as tall as he was. He knew he wouldn't grow any more, and he couldn't seem to put on much weight, either, but he wondered if she would grow more and end up being taller than him. Then he could look her right in the eye, when he wore his boots, and maybe if he sang "Per Spelemann," he could make her smile. That made him relax a little and just at the right time, because Clark burst out the door of the shed, off to return a scoop shovel to Torger Olson, and Lillie was standing in the doorway like she was framed in a picture.

He asked her for tea.

"Get it yourself," she said, and turned her back to him.

Somehow, seeing her back and the little curls already stuck to her neck this early in the morning—instead of those large, dark eyes—made it easier to follow her into the kitchen, where he picked his cup off the shelf and poured the last of the tea from the pot. He sat down at the small table where he could see her strong shoulders pulsing as she stabbed at the dirty clothes in the copper boiler of hot water with her washing bat.

"Where's that picture you promised me? The one of you?" he asked her. Picking at the old tobacco in his pipe with his knife, while he talked, made the question seem quite normal, but she ignored it.

"What happened to my father's sheep at Pomme de Terre that you were supposed to be taking care of?" she shot back at him. "You lost two lambs, too! You did!"

She wasn't really thinking about the sheep. She was thinking about this older man whose light blue eyes followed her every move in the kitchen when he sat at the table for supper. She regretted telling him about having her picture taken in town, because he thought he should have one, and that would feel like giving her very soul away to a strange man who couldn't even speak English properly.

She wanted him to go away. She wanted her neighbor Mrs. Risbrudt to walk in the door right now, since Mother and Charles were on their way to Fergus Falls. They wouldn't be home until late. She wanted to just get through the day without him staring at her, without his stupid, sing-song-y Norwegian accent ringing out, asking for more gravy, or coffee or anything at all! She hoped he would be in the potato field all day, and then in the barn, and then she would just put his supper out for him, and she would leave.

He felt bad about losing sheep, too, especially the lambs. But it was a big farm and there were a lot of sheep. The wolves found the sick ones before he did.

"That wasn't my fault," he said, but couldn't come up with anything more to say.

"You were paid to look after them! My father's prize sheep! It is your fault!"

"No, it 'twas the wolves, you see."

He said "wolves" with a "v." *Volves*. Couldn't even say it right.

She whirled to face him, just as he rose from the table, his pocketknife still open in his hand.

"So, do you have my picture?" he asked quietly, stepping toward her.

She grabbed the butcher knife from the counter and in a rush, as he took yet another step toward her, choked out, "Get out! Get out of here!" swiping at him with the knife that trembled in her soapy hand.

"My picture ..." he answered, bewildered and frightened, because she seemed that way, too. His face was flushed, and his stomach was turning over again. He was so embarrassed to be like this with her face just inches from his own. She must see every bead of sweat and his pale eyes melting into confusion.

Then she lunged at him, and his hands shot up—instinctively.

"Get out!" she screamed at him, tears and sweat bathing her red cheeks.

His right hand, the one holding his knife, still with bits of tobacco on it, flew out towards her, landing on her neck. She stopped screaming and the butcher knife slipped from her soap-slicked hands; she clutched at her neck and ran outside. She kept running, many feet from the doorway, but then she fell.

"*Å min Gud, min Gud!*" he said, following her to the place where she lay. Her face turned up to his, but there was no darkness in those eyes now. They were melting before him and more beautiful than he had ever seen them. But she was choking and couldn't breathe. He would not let a dog suffer so! And the knife found her throat once more.

Her damp cheeks turned pale as he knelt over her in wonder. What is this? What is this lifeless creature on the dirt path he walked just minutes before? *Min Gud! Min Gud! Min Gud!* ... My God.

The sun, now high overhead, made his head spin when he looked at it. He looked at the blinding blue sky; he looked back down at her; he looked over the fields with tiny sprouts dotting the deep, grey earth. She must be too warm, as he was, so he unbuttoned her skirt and her blouse and opened them up. With careful fingers, he touched the soft, pink skin below her neck and lingered there, but dared to touch nothing more.

She shouldn't stay here on this dirt path where anyone could see her. That much he sensed, but he didn't know where she belonged now. He thought and thought, until his eyes landed on the shaded grove in the pig lot. It would be cool there. The grass was thick and lush and would wrap around her like a sweet-smelling blanket. The sun went under a cloud, the air cooled slightly, and he reached his arms underneath her, lifted her to his lap and stood. She weighed about as much as a yearling calf, he thought, as he struggled over the rock pile and waded through the deep saw grass by the grove.

When he rolled her out of his arms to the ground, he was shocked by what was before him. A lifeless lump she was. Her clothes were wet and smelled bad. He took them off, even her stockings, which were wet and smelly, too. What else was inside her that would do this to her? This was not his Lillie! Not her! This bad smell, this pale color, these arms and legs draped in disorder over the rocks and branches also nesting in the grass ... what was this? His knife tore into the awful thing on the ground and with the expertise of a worthy farmhand, he split it front and back. He knew his butchering, he did, and made quick work of it.

When at last it did not seem like her at all, he turned his back and sat, respectfully, as one does in the presence of the dead. After what felt to him like an appropriate amount of time, he went to the lake, washed his hands and thought about what to do next. Thinking through problems had always been hard for him, but this was different. He couldn't even form a thought that seemed familiar, and therefore comforting. He didn't want to stay by the lake, or even at the farm. In fact, he didn't want to be here ever again—that much he knew—so he rose at last. When he saw how dirty his overalls were, he took them off, then took off his trousers, put on the overalls, and put his trousers over them. Now he didn't look so bad. He took a few

143

steps away from the lake, intending to head in the direction of Grant County and the house he'd lived in there, but someone might see him and ask what he was doing. He wouldn't know how to answer that, so he decided to stay by the lake until dark.

And Nels; where was he? A red-handed murderer, skulking from bush to bush, trying to flee from the scene of his awful crime!—Fergus Falls *Weekly Journal,* April 19, 1888

Nels Heads for Iowa, Later That Day

There was a lot to do this time of year. It didn't look good to be away—on foot and not working. With no horse, much less a wagon, it didn't look at all like he was working, so he just sat. The grass by the lake was already tall enough to almost hide him, sitting there. If he lay down, even Clark wouldn't find him right away, if the boy came down here to look for frogs. So Nels lay down, but when he closed his eyes, he heard Lillie yelling, "You're a bad man!" and he sat up, right away, and he stayed that way for a long time.

He wanted to figure out what happened, but thinking was so hard. He was grateful for the season's first mosquitos pestering him as the sun finally got a little lower and the breeze faded to nothing. Then he thought about the mosquitos and not Lillie. He still wasn't tired, but he was getting hungry as the sun slipped behind the western slope of the lake, and so he stood up to go ... somewhere.

He headed south, avoiding the Olson place. Clark might still be there. Mrs. Olson fed the boy bread and cheese and let him play with their dogs. Once beyond the neighbors, he picked his way along proper roads with no grass left down the middle, and the bits of field roads packed down from a team. It wasn't the fastest way, but he didn't want to see anybody or talk to anybody.

When he passed Lake Sewell, he mostly just took the roads. It surely would have been easy to spot him, if anybody had known to look: a lone figure outlined in the last light of dusk, striding along the road, his head disappearing over the crest of one hill and popping up at the top of the next. He decided to go to Charles' Pomme de Terre farm. He liked it there. He kept a few things there, too, like his overcoat. He might need that, and he wouldn't want to show up in Iowa without it, since it was really his brother's.

Thinking about what else he might have left at Charles' farm occupied his mind for a bit longer, but there wasn't much, and soon the image of Lillie's hand grasping her own neck was so clear that he stumbled off the road and wandered along the ditch for a ways. It was the look on her face—not pain, exactly. He'd never seen anyone's face like that that he could remember—her mouth open and the corners of her pale lips turned down, her large dark eyes scrunched into slits like a cat just falling asleep, her forehead full of wrinkles he didn't know she had. She was too young to look that way, and it terrified him. She shouldn't have scared him like that.

Dust rose above the next hill, which told him a wagon was going to go right past him, so he just sat down in the long grass and waited for it to go by. The closer he got to the Pomme de Terre farm, the more he wished to be alone. The coming night was a comfort. He struggled with a most unfamiliar pain and longed to sit at his mother's table again. She might shake her finger at him when he pushed a potato onto his fork with his thumb, but then she'd rest her large, strong hand on his shoulder, and he'd smile like the boy he really was.

Stars were splashed above him everywhere he looked when he climbed over the fence at Standal's place to the north of Charles' farm. He could wander as he wished along the shore of Field Lake. It was very pretty with the trees all leafed out, and the moon playing across a little chop on the water. Columbine bloomed in the open patches; blue and white flowers had popped up in the damp areas along the shore. He didn't know the names of those. He would have picked flowers for Lillie every day, but with that thought, his knees folded underneath him, dropping him like a clump at the bottom of a maple tree. Its lower branches curled down like a big umbrella over his crumpled frame.

He watched the maple's big, jagged leaves with red veins flit in front of his face, but with the moonlight slashing through the woods like that, they looked too much like the part of Lillie that had been cut—all jagged and threaded with veins—so he got up, steadied himself on the tree trunk, then took a few more steps and leaned on another tree. This is how he made his way to the little house where he hoped to find some food, spend the night, and go on to Wendell where he could get a train home to Iowa the next day.

After the boy played awhile at Mr. Olson's, he went to another neighbor, Mr. Lerwick, where he remained for a while and then came home. No one was there. Nels was gone; Lilly was nowhere to be seen. He played around until night, waiting for Lilly to return. But no Lilly came.
—Fergus Falls *Weekly Journal*, April 19, 1888

Clark and the Kittens, Early Evening

Past suppertime, the sun would be slipping around the west edge of the house and dropping behind the trees soon. He knew that somewhere beyond the trees was Fergus Falls, because that's the direction his mother and his big brother went early that morning. It was a warm day late in the spring, and there was plenty to do. There were lots of frogs on the grassy edge of the lake. If he could sit still long enough, he could watch them catch damsel flies and eat 'em, but it was more fun to chase garter snakes, and if he got lucky, one of them would eat a frog.

But now it was too dark. He'd already been all the way to the Olson's and Lerwick's, too, and he was hungry, so he went to the house. When he was little, like three or four, his mother let him strike the match and light the lamp when it got too dark in the house for her to wash up after supper—but only when she was right there with him. She said you could start the whole house on fire if you didn't know what you were doing with those matches. So, he knew how to light a lamp. He used to see his father light it, too, then light his pipe and lie on the settee with his legs dangling over the end. Mother hated that. It was her nice settee, she said.

That was before he saw the thing wearing Father's clothes dangling from the beam in the hayloft. He didn't know what it was. It looked so scary. The barn door opened. A quick breeze raced through, and the beam creaked when the door slammed against the barn wall. It was Mother. The thing hanging with Father's clothes on moved, and when it moved it squeaked.

He used to love the hayloft where the barn cats hid their kittens, but now he didn't like it as much. It was easy to find them because they mewed real loud. He knew if Father found them, he'd give them away, or tie them in an old feed sack full of rocks and throw them in the lake, but not the mother cat. They had to have a couple cats around to "get rid of those goddam mice and gophers," Father said.

Clark was good at finding the kittens before Father; usually they were burrowed into a cave in the hay. The mother cat always ended up moving them again, sometimes right under Father's nose. Cats aren't that smart, but after Father was gone, there was no need to save them. So now they had lots of cats, but no Father.

He lit the lamp, pulled the bread down from the cutting board on the table and stretched out on the settee with the half-loaf of bread to wait for Lillie, or the hired man, or just somebody to come home. If his mother were there in the kitchen, he would see the thin line of dust that coated the hem of her dress. It was nice to think about it. When she bent down to pick up the tails of a shirt in the basket under the clothesline, her hem dipped in the dirt. He knew that's where the dirt came from because the kitchen floor was always clean.

He took a big bite of the bread and thought about the kittens in the lake and the smell of the lake when it bloomed in late summer when the frogs were quiet. He thought of the round, brown eyes of the deer that drank from it, standing at its edge, just close enough to sip. If he sat still, upwind, they didn't know he was there, thinking about the kittens. He fell asleep before he'd half-chewed his next bite of bread.

147

At sunrise Charles Field arose to prepare for the labors of the day. He went to the barn to feed the horses and he found the stock just as he had left it on the previous morning and evidently without having been fed. He at once started to the field where he had told Holong to plant potatoes before leaving for Fergus, to see what he had done. The field had not been disturbed. The nearest way to the house was through a small pasture of 8 or 10 acres, known as the hog lot. —Fergus Falls *Weekly Journal,* April 19, 1888

Iver Lerwick: Lillie is Discovered, Friday, May 27, 1887

Lillie was a strong girl, tall for fifteen. But still, you'd think Charles could have picked her up by himself, Iver Lerwick thought as he hurried to the Field's farm near his own. The message—that Lillie was found dead—was just awful, and he wondered at the circumstance, as Charles had told him nothing more but to come quick. So, he did, and was not prepared for what he saw.

Charles was in the grove, crumpled on his knees holding his sister's head in his hands and staring at the wreckage of her naked body, torn apart, her torso ripped to pieces. His shotgun lay in the grass nearby next to a dead pig.

Iver said nothing for many seconds, so shocked was he. Finally, he recognized that somebody must do something, and he took off his coat and laid it on the matted grass, instructing Charles to help lift Lillie onto it. Iver was grateful he still had work gloves on. It was unthinkable that he would touch her bare, bloody flesh with his calloused hands, though the concern for such delicacies under the circumstances was senseless. Blood and body fluids were gone, soaked into the lumpy earth beneath her—or some nocturnal creature's dinner. Unless it was that pig. The thought brought his breakfast up in his throat; he had to struggle to suck in a breath and force it back down.

He'd butchered plenty of wild game and farm animals. The similarity gave him something else to think about as he gently folded the skin over her open torso, as best he could. It was so jagged and loose that it was a mostly pointless gesture. The idea was to make her look more like a whole person—and quickly. Charles was ashen and had not spoken since Iver had arrived on the scene.

"Charles, together now. You lift that end," Iver told him. "Are you ready?"

Charles didn't move.

"Charles?" he asked. "Can you lift her from that end? ... We can't leave her here."

Charles finally lifted his eyes to meet Iver's. They were brimming with tears that had yet to fall. "No, we can't, can we," he answered at last, and with difficulty pulled himself up in a kneeling position, gathered her arms over what was left of her chest, and shoved his arms under her shoulders. He was trembling so bad he could barely hang on.

But it got worse. When they tried to lift her onto the coat, they found she'd been opened up all the way down the back, too, and she was falling apart right in their arms. Charles set his teeth, shoved his arms around as much of her as he could reach, his face even with what was left of her insides, and with a roar, heaved her on to the coat. Iver quickly wrapped it around her and bolted to his side, just in time to shove him into a slightly drier patch of grass nearby, where his body wretched and heaved but brought nothing up but stinking liquid.

Finally, it stopped, and Charles rose to his feet. He grabbed Iver's arm, but just for a second or two. "All right," he said. "Let's get her out of here," and spit behind him into the grass.

"What kind of ... of ... monster ...?" The question just escaped from Iver, and he stopped himself.

"I know ... I know who," Charles answered.

With Lillie gathered up in the coat, he could manage on his own, picking his way around the piles of hog manure and over the deadfall.

"You sure …?" Iver started to say.

"I got her," Charles said, and strode to the granary, away from their mother, who was still asleep in her room.

4. The Face of the Law, Fergus Falls, May 28

Sheriff Alonzo Brandenburg had a little time for once, so he decided to see what was at the bottom of the pile on his desk. The newspaper report of his election was flattened among several other clippings. His wife, Alice, took great pleasure in saving any mention of him in the newspapers—the Fergus Falls *Journal*, particularly.

"Mr. Underwood is the one with influence, don't you think?" She'd tell him. Yes, he did think. … It paid to stay on the Journal publisher's good side. Given his name, it was easy to understand why Underwood figured he was German, and Alonzo didn't see any reason to correct him. In fact, his parents were both born in Norway, and even though he had never seen the land of his heritage, he carried a fondness for all things Norwegian. Alonzo leaned back at last, put his boots up on his desk and pulled on his moustache, scratching around for bits of the bread that might be left there from his breakfast.

Thinking.

He'd enjoyed an uneventful couple of years that first term. His deputy Steve Butler had handled much of what was controversial since the only murders were in Steve's corner of the county. Perham. Rowdy place.

He was also grateful that he lived in Fergus—and grateful for Butler, too. Good man. Now if Brandenburg could just get the village of Elizabeth to settle down, he could breathe a little easier. Then it was 1886, and every day, it seemed, he had asked himself, "What in tarnation happened?" Alice Kempfer finally got herself rid of Barney, but then Barney got rid of Smith, who wasn't much of a lawyer, but you had to credit him with getting Alice out of that house. Barney should've been locked up—at least for his own good—but the fine people of this county didn't see fit to do that and let the drunkard go.

Elizabeth just wasn't like Fergus. Just down the road, but … well … unpredictable. It made him jumpy. First Smith was shot, then Lulu Harris. Ned Wilson had made a monkey out of law enforcement, but nobody cared much that Wilson did himself in, least of all Brandenburg. Saved the county the trouble and expense of a trial. With Lulu's reputation, it would have been a circus.

The sheriff was more comfortable with routine and cases he understood: a farmer asking after his teenage daughter who fled her job in town. Mostly the hired girls ended up going home—or took off west for good. Gambling was rampant downtown at all hours, but closing those games down was like shootin' rats; there were always more. Still, Underwood expected him to try. If Alonzo fed him enough stories detailing his occasional success, everybody would be satisfied.

Otherwise, just a few accidental deaths to investigate, spats between neighbors, a rare suicide. Now, Alphonso Field's suicide ... that was another matter. Downright strange, that was. Couldn't figure it at all, even though the old guy was flighty, like the *Journal* said. There was plenty the sheriff saw that didn't quite add up, but only so much worth chasing. Lots of folks doing foolish things—mostly to make a few bucks selling liquor without a license. But not St. Olaf township where the Fields lived. Never had much trouble come out of St. Olaf.

Alonzo let out a big yawn, stretched and dropped his feet back to the floor. The chair creaked so loud, it woke him up enough to notice the boy from the telegraph office dashing across the street waving a message in his hand. He was headed right for Brandenburg's door. Something about the boy's red face and the way he clutched that message ... told Alonzo his quiet morning had come to an end, and his heart beat a little faster.

The alarm sounded quick enough. Coroner Bedford was the first contacted, after Charles told his neighbor Torger Olson. Between Torger and Iver Lerwick, there were folks who knew before Sheriff Brandenburg had even telegraphed towns nearby to alert everyone—law enforcement or no—that there was a killer on the loose. Posses were sent in various directions Friday night.

The Otter Tail County Coroner's Sworn Statement
May 28, 1887

OFFICE OF
SHERIFF OF OTTER TAIL COUNTY,

———

A. BRANDENBURG,
SHERIFF

W. C. Bedford sworn as witness says am coroner of this Co. Made an examination on body of Lillian Field the 27th of May at residence of Mrs. Field at St. Olaf in Otter Tail County ... found remains lying in out building wrapped up in a blanket in a grainery ... the body was blackened by dust—throat cut—incision____ down to her bones. Incision _____ done with a knife or some short instrument. There was a gash at_____. Also a long cut in back. Generally—the _____were removed—the _____ gaped down and open about 7(?) inches. The wound made by the cut had severed all the main arteries in her throat. The left hand was all right— the right hand was lacerated—The _____ _____from injury—a long bruise on left arm (?) and _____ back side of head—discolored— also on the neck. A longer bruise—hair matted—no fractures of limbs that I discovered—Girl was _____ 5ft 5-4 to _____ - slender—would weigh about 105-110 pounds and frame—rather small—limbs(?) were developed—hair brown—light complexion—good looking in my opinion her death was caused by incision (?) knife wounds—bled to death. —W. C. Bedford. [vi]

Walter Preston Apprehends Nels

Walter Preston, who lived near Ashby, which was near the Field's Pomme de Terre farm, had a feeling that if Brandenburg had just stopped and asked folks who knew about this Holong fella, the sheriff would know exactly where to go. Nels was a little funny in the head and had no more ability to escape than a squirrel in a root cellar. Walter Preston knew that Nels had spent a few months at Field's Pomme de Terre farm in Grant County. Nels had a friend from down home in Iowa who lived in the village of Wendell to the west. Wendell also had a train depot, and Nels was most likely to try to catch the train headed south. Either that, or Ashby to the east. That's what Walter thought.

"And I only knew what I picked up from folks," he told the sheriff. "It was me who first struck up the trail. Not by accident, as I said."

Sure enough, Holong had high tailed it right back to that Pomme de Terre farm and a man Walter didn't know, but who he had met on the road, said he'd seen a fella answering to the description of Holong headed towards Wendell on foot. That would've been later Friday.

Walter and a neighbor, Jake Heald, headed out and got to Wendell just before daybreak on Saturday. Jake thought Holong might have headed for the boxcars lined up on the train tracks at the depot in Wendell, so he started sneaking around 'em with his right hand on his pistol, like he's stalking some desperado. Walter couldn't help laughing, even though he knew what Holong had done and all.

No trains were moving at the moment, so Walter sat down on the rail to shake the sand outa his boots, when his eyes set on a house not far from the depot. There was a light inside.

"Jake!" Walter called out. "C'mon!" and Jake hurried to him. "See that house? I just got a feeling about it."

"Olson's, right? Ain't he Norwegian, too?" Jake asked. "Let's go," and the pair set off in the direction of the house.

Turns out there was a little barn behind it, and the door was open. Walter was watching the door, when someone broke wind so loud that Walter heard him before the small man with his trousers over his overalls came around the corner of the barn. The two stood, looking at each other for just a second or two—Holong with a sheepish expression on his face.

"It was Holong, all right. He started to run," Walter related to the sheriff. "But Jake Heald came around the other side of the barn, and when we told him to stop, he did. Holong asked if he could get the overcoat he'd left at the depot, so we let'm, and we started for Ashby. We'd gone about a mile, and I asked him if he knew that the Field girl was dead. He said that he did, and he had killed her."

Saving the Suspect

Early Saturday morning he [Sheriff Brandenburg] found parties who told him that Walter Preston of Ashby had arrested him at Wendell and had just passed by on his way to Ashby. The sheriff at once took charge of him. It was feared that violence might be attempted, but no demonstration was made, perhaps on account of the early hours of the morning. —Fergus Falls *Weekly Journal*, Thursday, June 2, 1887.

... Before anyone knew that Holong had been captured he was safe in jail. It was well that he was. The horrible atrocity of the crime was sufficient to arouse any community, but in addition to this was the fact that no murderer in Otter Tail County had ever been punished in the slightest degree, save Tibbets, who was lynched at Perham. There were serious threats to lynch him, but the better sentiment prevailed upon the assurance of the authorities that he would be punished in due time. —Fergus Falls *Weekly Journal*, November 17, 1887, as reported at the time of the trial.

Sheriff Brandenburg watched the man sitting across from him in the box car. There was no time to wait for a passenger train to haul his prisoner safely back to the county jail. The countryside was roiling with talk—and anger. Most folks knew the Fields. They were good farmers and decent folks, and they'd suffered enough, God knows, what with Alphonso's hanging himself and Esther and the baby dying. "Poor Priscilla," Brandenburg had heard about a dozen times already that morning.

But the man sitting there had the look of a schoolboy who slouched in the back of the room and hoped the teacher wouldn't call on him. There was nothing frightening about him, except that the Sheriff had the story.

"I didn't vant to go d'er, yew know," he said to Brandenburg. "It vasn't a happy house d'ere. I stay down here in Grant County and den tings be okay. Yah, vell … Dose Fields!

"Nels, you can't tell me that poor girl had it coming."

I tell ya! It vasn't no good place to be! Not so good, no!"

And so it went. Nels going on about the Fields and then sitting in silence, connected only loosely to the limited activity around him, noticing the lurch of the train approaching a hill and the groan of the couplers as it descended on the other side, but little else.

Brandenburg watched him and thought about the Field girl. He had never had the chance to see a child grow up. His wife had but one baby, who died as an infant. Taking in his mother-in-law and his wife's younger siblings gave him a family. Maybe that was better than what Priscilla was going through right now, but he couldn't imagine it. None of it was better or worse. It was all just senseless to him.

Holong seemed oblivious to where this train—and his own future—were going, his pale blue eyes empty and lost, like a summer sky with no clouds to define it. He came back around only to rant about the Fields, and then seemed to "disappear" again.

The train rattled on towards Fergus Falls. Brandenburg would have the fella locked up before anybody knew where he was, just the way he'd hoped it would go. It wouldn't do to have another lynching in Otter Tail County. It had enough black marks with the state. Never been a killer punished, but Brandenburg had a feeling in his gut that the dubious honor was going to fall to him.

The workings of the county's legal system, such as it was, would proceed as the state had legislated that it must; the newspaper would glory in every detail about the killing, the victim, the prisoner, and the testimony at the trial as it marched to its inevitable conclusion. This scenario might just as well have been passing in front of his eyes as the train chugged closer to town, the jail, the coming outcry among the citizenry and the final page that the sheriff alone could write. Nels

Holong was his prisoner, in his county and it was his lever to pull on the scaffold that he would have to build.

The car smelled of leather. And blood. Must have hauled hides. Brandenburg rose to open the car's wide door a bit and grab some fresh air. Every field had evidence of being turned over and most were planted. He usually loved spring. This year would be different. This year, the small figure hunched in the corner of the rail car, not making the smallest effort to escape, this person of no consequence, prior to his horrific crime, could define his year, consume the Sheriff's activities and thoughts, and even write his legacy in the history of this county.

He saw it all through the crack in the door, as the waves of pasture grass and wildflowers passed in front of him, blurred, and then detached from his field of vision. Lillie Field's case was less than a day old and weighed on him as if he'd never known life without it.

The Prisoner: *When the sheriff alighted from the train, no one would have imagined that he had a man capable of such a fiendish deed with him. Holong looks like a simple minded Norwegian ... he evinced no fear and very little concern ... When Sheriff Brandenburg was asked in his presence if there had been any attempt to hang him at Ashby, Holong looked with surprise that such a thing was possible. He hardly seems to realize the enormity of his crime, or else he is a stoic.*

The Victim: *The victim of this horrible crime was said to be a very pretty girl with plump round features, rather large for her age. She was an American, her family being one of the few in that town. She was quite a strong girl and unless killed, as outlined by her murderer, must have struggled hard for her honor and life.* —Fergus Falls *Weekly Journal*, June 2, 1887.

Charles, Later That Day

From what he and others have said, it is plain that he was under the impression he loved the girl, and annoyed her a good deal with his attentions. She, however, took no notice of him. ... He says he liked her from the first time he saw her ...

Charles snapped the newspaper shut and flung it at the kindling box. Enough. How is it that everyone in the county, it seemed, knew more about Holong than he did? "Don't leave me!" she had shrieked as the wagon carried them away that morning. He'd laughed. Mother had just nodded and shook her finger over the reins in his hand. Drive on. ...

My God.

Ingeborg and Kittel: Brother and Sister, June 1887

She waited on a bench by the door. Her brother, Kittel, was off talking to the lawyer; he couldn't bring himself to face his brother yet. He didn't tell her this, but he didn't have to. The jail was fairly new, but it was most certainly not clean. She determined it would be necessary to sit very still so as not to rub the dust into her traveling costume.

"Nels is using the, uh ... pot," she was told. She could hear him pissing behind the wall against her back. The smell added to the indignity of this place, its dusty plank floors, its wavy glass windowpanes, the smoke hanging in the air, fresh puffs curling around the corner of the wall.

She didn't know Nels smoked. She didn't like it much, so it was yet another disappointing thing about her younger brother, and another indication that he had not grown up very much. Their father smoked a proper pipe. Young, wild boys smoked cig'rettes. Her brother was not wild—or young. The smoke haze mixed with the fading scent of warm pee was enough of a distraction to keep her composed, for which she was thankful.

The trip up from Iowa had been agonizing. She'd spent the better part of it crying, while Kittel clenched and unclenched his fists, crossed and uncrossed his legs, stared out the window, told her to try to get some sleep, then started the rigmarole all over again. If she broke off a piece of *lefse* for him, he'd take it with small interest, manage one bite, and then hold it, staring

158

out the window, the lefse pinched between his thumb and fingers, pieces crumbling on his trousers. The sight of it set her crying anew. That was their lives right now. Crumbling.

The train clattered on. Passengers alighted, boarded, tromped up and down the aisles ... "S'cuse me" ... "May I?" Then stuffed a bag on the shelf over their seat, coat flapping in her face. She wrapped her arms around her small traveling case and offered a small nod. Kittel scowled, and the passenger sat across the aisle, noting their lack of interest in conversation. Kittel thought *he* should sit on the aisle, but she wanted to be able to stand up and move about as she wished. Sitting still was unbearable, as the weight of the crime of which her brother was accused took hold of her again and again. She tried to pray but could think of nothing to say after "*Kjære Far i himmelen,*" pressing her handkerchief over her damp eyes. Again ... "Dear Father in heaven ..."

"We must save him, you know," Kittel said after a long stint of staring. "Father ... *Dette kan drepe han.*" He took a bite of lefse.

Yes, it could kill him. It's killing me, Ingeborg stood up. She stood up and headed for the door at the end of the car, gripping the backs of the seats on either side of the aisle as the car lurched arrhythmically from side to side. She couldn't bear to sit there and witness Kittel's suffering, any more than she could inflict her own on him. If she could have hurled herself out the door of the train and rolled down the embankment to another time and place, she would have leaped with gratitude. Every death she had endured came roaring back upon her. Her little brother, Peder, gone at six years old. Her twins dead just days after they were born ... her own little Peder, just hours.

She flung the door open and let the rush of warm air dry her tear-soaked cheeks. "Ole, Ole! I need you now!" she cried out, but all that did was to bring her back to her husband's graveside—she, with her arms wrapped around little Maline, fixated on the fresh dirt sprinkled on his coffin. She knew her little girl was not strong, but never did she think she'd lose her, too, in little more than a month.

Nels must not hang! He must not! She, as much as anybody, had already saved his life twice. He was just as sick as Peder—and a year younger—but somehow, he survived, although Ingeborg marked his questioning gazes and lack of attention. He hadn't been confirmed yet, and a rambunctious colt brought him to the brink again.

When Nels came to, Kittel joked, "*Toff gutt,* our Nels."

But it was no joke. Nels may have seemed a tough boy, even after a kick in the head by a horse. But something was not right with him.

"Ma'am?" a voice said, and her eyes wandered across the floor to a pair of worn but polished leather boots. She looked up to see a man about her age, she imagined, with a bushy moustache. "I'm Sheriff Brandenburg. You want to see him now?"

Still heavy with thoughts of home, she rose and followed the Sheriff around the partial wall to see Nels putting out another cig'rette in a small tin of sand. It was full of used ones. The Sheriff let her into the cell, pulled the door shut until it clicked tight, and went to the desk in the corner.

"Oh, Nels!" she cried, and threw her arms around the man before her. The tears were unstoppable now, accompanied by gasping sobs. She could barely breathe. At last, he put his arms around her too, because he thought that's what she would expect of him.

"*Hvor er Far?*" he asked.

"Iowa. *Han oppbevare gården.*" She could barely manage the words. She knew their father was disconsolate by this news. The farm work was saving him. For now.

"*Ja. … ja. Hvordan er Mor?*"

"*Ikke så verste.*" Not so bad. … That wasn't altogether true. Their mother was so mortified that she hadn't left the house. What could she say to anyone? She did not sleep either, so terrified was she to think she could lose her son, and if she lost him, she would lose her husband, too. She knew it. But Nels must know none of this. He needed to believe that there was hope.

160

Sheriff Brandenburg was grateful it had been a blessedly quiet summer following Holong's arrest, and that the county commissioners had funded building a new jail in '85. Trying to keep the jail up for the parade of curious folks, who concocted excuses for visiting Nels Holong, kept Jake too busy, but having a jailor at all was a blessing, so Brandenburg was grateful for Jake, too.

However, he found it irksome to have the responsibility of holding anybody for months, waiting for district court. Jake tried to keep the drunken overnighters away from Nels, which cut down on the bullying neither one of them—Jake or the Sheriff—could abide.

So, it was busy, but manageable. Then late in October the Lucy boys got into a drunken fracas in Henning and killed a man. But in little more than a month, Eugene Lucy's trial and sentencing were over and done, and with a lifetime prison sentence, he could put that whole business in the state's lap.

It was a sad case, but it didn't plague him the way the sight of those bloody overalls did when he stripped Nels down after his arrest. Months later, and he still couldn't get the sight of it out of his mind. He'd catch himself watching his prisoner while he talked with a visitor, trying to figure out what went on in that poor, dumb Norwegian's head. He honestly believed that Nels had told the truth. But … why?

Nels Olson Holong, Murderer of Lilly Field, Indicted for Murder in The First Degree: *The grand jury returned its first indictment Tuesday, which was against Nels Olson Holong, who murdered Lilly Field in St. Olaf last spring. The indictment was for murder in the first degree. The rumors which have been somewhat prevalent that there were accomplices, or that he had been induced by others to commit the crime, were thoroughly looked into by County Attorney Lewis, and not the least foundation was found for any of them. Judge Baxter assigned Rawson & Houpt as attorneys to defend him and he was arraigned at the opening of court Tuesday afternoon.* —Fergus Falls *Journal,* November 17, 1887.

Bert Rawson, Esq., Attorney for the Defense: Shut up, Nels!

"Oh, good God! How does one get through to this ... this ... this ... man-child?" Bert Rawson shouted across the dinner table. His wife, Nettie, endured his occasional rants about local politics and such, but this had his face red with exasperation, and he hadn't even been drinking, for a change. Gravy splattered on the lace tablecloth when he dropped his fork on his plate.

"He had to do nothing at all but keep his mouth shut, and it would be a damn sight harder to prove first degree. That stuffed shirt Lewis would have to do some real work to earn his county paycheck! This Holong fella's handing them the guilty verdict they could never get with competence, pure and simple, regardless of the merits of the case. Failure after failure."

Nettie busied herself cleaning up around little Horace's plate. Bert folded his arms, wrapping himself up in his own brand of self-righteousness. He had never let the merits of a case hold him back, and he'd defended some jackasses. Drunk and disorderly ... gambling on Sunday ... that one made him laugh. Why the hell would Lewis—or Judge Baxter, for that matter—concern themselves with his fuddled chums? Let a guy drink and play dice if he wants! Good God! Half of the defense work was convincing the judge that you believed what you were saying—easy with the parade of nonsense cases the county attorney threw at him. He was proud of getting Barney Kempfer off, though. Drinking is one thing, but that man had a real problem.

"Then I get to defend *this* jackass!" he said under his breath, slapping his hands on the table.

"Well, dear ..." Nettie had a carefully thought-out comment, but Bert wasn't done yet.

"And his family thinks that I will rescue their idiotic brother from the fate he sealed for himself! Good GOD!"

Nettie dropped her thought, rose from the table and cleared their plates. She loved him for his passion—that's how she

162

thought of it—for taking on cases and standing up to the powers-that-be. The dishes clattering woke the baby, and she hurried to comfort little Helen. Four-year-old Horace was building something on the kitchen floor with kindling from the wood box and blessedly paid no mind.

With his plate gone, Bert plunked his arms on the table—heedless of the spilled gravy—drummed his fingers and brooded. All-overish … that's how he felt, and it wasn't like him. He couldn't bring himself to despise Nels Holong, and he had to do what he could to save his sorry ass, if for no other reason than his general distain for Lewis, Underwood, Baxter and, by association, Brandenburg, who wasn't such a bad sort, but he'd fallen in with Bert's nemeses, so he was one of them. They thought they ran the town—and the county, too, or at least the western part of it. They couldn't be bothered with spending much time in Perham and the eastern half. Too bad because they'd had chances for convictions in that area. Idiots. No "sand."

These were things that he could bellow to his wife at home, but he was infinitely more frustrated in his office and on the streets of Fergus Falls, much less in the courthouse, where he kept it to himself, lest he lose the county income he'd managed to snag. He knew why he had been appointed to this case. He was going to lose, and those buggers loved to see him lose.

The indictment, Coroner Bedford's report, the grand jury testimony, Holong's supposed legitimate confession to Sheriff Brandenburg—it all played over and over in his head, as the rattling of dishes ended in the kitchen and his wife murmuring to their infant daughter took over. He had, at last, had a conversation with his client, and at that point, Rawson had just one thing to say to him: "Shut up, Nels. Just shut up."

But it was too late. The county had assembled more than enough proof to proceed. The legal locomotive had gathered steam quickly, and everyone—from the townships to Fergus Falls itself—had jumped onboard and was full of righteous indignant energy. Bert already knew that he had but one slim chance: an insanity plea, if Holong hadn't dynamited that possibility, too, with his description of the crime, events leading up to it and his actions following it. He even corrected details when his inquisitors got them wrong. "Shut the fuck up!" he whispered across the empty table.

Rawson had never known such a puzzle as Nels Holong. Could he be that stupid? If he was, how did he get that little kid out of the way, pull off this horrendous murder, and just walk away? Something wasn't right about the whole damn thing.

Nettie had the kitchen cleaned up and Horace tucked into bed when Bert pulled himself up from the table, stretched, yawned, and headed outside to the front steps of their house. It was a pleasant evening for November. No wind. He could certainly walk downtown and have a drink or two with the boys, but he was so on edge … He didn't feel like joking around about this idiot Holong, either. None a' their damn business.

The fresh air brought some relief, and the stars gave him something gloriously beyond Fergus Falls to consider. Nettie appeared and settled in next to him, sighing a little too loud as she dropped to the step, wrapping a thick, wool shawl around her.

"You know, dear," she started.

"Don't," he answered.

"His sister …"

"She doesn't see what this could cost her family."

"That's to her credit, isn't it?"

"Is it? They don't know what they are facing in this town." He looked down at his sleeping baby girl, and they were quiet for a time. "She was just fifteen years old," he said, staring into his tiny daughter's peaceful face.

"Well, he's crazy," Nettie said. "I should think that's quite obvious."

"Doesn't matter. It's already decided, Nettie. But I will try to save him from hanging."

"But the judge—or the jury—can decide that I thought."

"No longer the case. The State has changed the law again. First degree ... there's no discretion. Lewis and Bedford were positively gleeful when they filed the complaint. They were laughing, Nettie! I'm going to lose the case, and they know it. They're finally going to get their hanging, but of course they're not going to have to carry it out. That's why Brandenburg was even more quiet than usual."

The baby let out a little cry, and Nettie pulled the huge shawl around her. Bert wandered over to the lilac bushes that were just bare sticks this time of year.

He never let his cases bother him, but they mostly involved getting people off for stupid liquor violations and such. This was something else entirely.

"But if he actually did this horrible deed, dear," she started to ask.

"There's something not right about this—there's something not right about *him!*" he said and snapped off a dry twig. Helen let out a squawk and Nettie offered the startled baby some comfort nursing.

Bert watched them for a moment and turned away, tilting his head up toward the deep indigo sky. "And I am suckin' hind tit," he said under his breath.

... He was brought into court by Jailor Jacobson. This is the first time he has been out of doors since the day after the murder, and as he was led from the jail to the courthouse he glanced in every direction, as if he enjoyed the outside world once more. ... He has grown quite thin and pale with his confinement. ... His married sister, who is older, and a brother are here from Decorah, Iowa, and had a conference with him in the jail before he was brought into court, although his sister was present when the indictment was read. —Fergus Falls *Weekly Journal,* November 17.

5. The Trial and Aftermath, November 21–22, 1887

The attorneys for the defense were somewhat tardy in arriving and the court sent an officer after them. After waiting twenty minutes Mr. Noben, one of the attorneys, appeared and the court ordered the trial to begin, refusing to wait longer for Mr. Rawson, the chief counsel. Fortunately, Mr. Rawson soon came in and the work of impaneling a jury was begun. — Fergus Falls *Weekly Journal,* Thursday, November 24.

Rawson really doubted whether Nobin, who calls himself a lawyer, could pick a jury out of a pickle barrel. "Stall! Stall! Come up with something! Do you have no imagination at all?" Bert was thinking when he had bounded up the courthouse steps. Bert Rawson strode into the courtroom, nodding at Holong's brother Kittil who stood up and turned to look when the heavy door at the back of the courtroom crashed open.

God, if they only knew … He'd spent all night losing at poker and drinking bad whiskey for that idiot Holong. If he could win the saloons, he had a shot to win.

"He's not right in the head, I tell ya!" Bert said, and folded another hand, holding a pair. "He ain't no more responsible than that drunk Barney Kempfer. This ain't no first degree. This is passion, my friend! Heat a' the moment!"

That was good stuff, and no matter how they attempted to sequester the jury, it would get around. Talk on the street was strong medicine, and enough of it would cure the hanging fever that goddam Underwood at the goddam *Journal* had been spreading since Holong spilled his story. There was always more to a story when Underwood told it, but this wasn't a game of who was going to win first; it was about who would win the biggest. If Holong hung for it, Rawson intended to plant enough doubts about his sanity and the wisdom of a first-degree conviction that this town would see a new hero in their corner by the next mayoral election. He almost had all the boys in the saloons and backrooms. That was easier since they were always getting into scrapes and needed his services.

Getting to court on time—that was the hard part for Rawson. "My apologies, Your Honor," he said when he caught his breath and sat down.

Judge Baxter never liked him much. Hind tit again. He glanced back at Kittel who was still standing. The look on his face said it all: That's no way to win over a jury, boys.

At 2 o'clock County Attorney Lewis opened the case for the state. ... He called the attention of the jury to the fact that no murderer had ever been convicted in this county and that it was a by-word throughout the state. —Fergus Falls *Weekly Journal,* November 24, 1887.

"Here we go," Rawson thought. "Let's make this pathetic little Norwegian from Iowa pay for all our stinkin' blunders. Nobin had an earnest look on his face and was scribbling on a piece of paper in the odd upside-down way that left-handers have. He had barely acknowledged Rawson since they had had words the night before. It had been building up, and frankly Rawson felt better after letting off a little steam. Nobin was ridiculously proper about his insults. "I beg your pardon!" was about the toughest language he could manage.

C.B. [Charles] Field was called. "... He was a good farm hand, faithful and attended to his work. I left him in charge of my stock. I consider him of fair intelligence; he never showed any signs of being out of his head or of being an imbecile."—Fergus Falls *Weekly Journal,* November 24, 1887.

Nobin was too close to the case and Rawson knew it ... friends of the family back in Iowa, and a pretty good friend of Kittel's, he'd heard. That was not the way to deal with legal matters, but if Holong's family wanted another attorney on Nels' case, and were willing to pay Nobin, that's their business.

Rawson was happy to build his case for mayor of the county seat, which would infuriate Judge Baxter and the rest of the county's pompous-ass Bar. He could hardly keep from laughing out loud, but Priscilla Field had just stepped down after her useless sworn testimony and that kind of disrespect was unthinkable. Even Bert Rawson knew that.

Still ... he wanted to know a few things that only Mrs. Field was likely to know. Even if she was blameless from every conceivable vantage point, she may very well have shed some light on Lillie's state of mind concerning old man Field's suicide, and the girl's feelings about Holong's interest in her, but she didn't, and Rawson figured he had no choice but to leave her alone. So, Mrs. Field sat, pale and quivering, surrounded by family and friends.

Judge Baxter was squinting at him over his glasses, but Bert was still thinking: *What, exactly, did Lillie say to her mother and brother before they left that morning? Anything? Did she argue with them the night before? What about? What did they tell her? Wouldn't the judge and the jury want to know?*

The look on Baxter's face was abundantly clear. No. They didn't want to know.

They had their culprit and that was—quite literally—all that mattered.

Rawson said, "No questions, Your Honor."

Clark Field, the 6-year-old boy, was then put on the stand, and showed that he was quite bright by his answers. His story was just as he told it last spring, and agrees with what Holong told a Journal reporter on the day of the capture. —Fergus Falls *Weekly Journal*, November 24, 1887.

"Who puts a six-year-old on the stand? Good God. Then Torger Olson ... he didn't know any more than the little kid. ..." Bert was thinking. He was relieved that he had insisted Nobin open their case. Nobin was likely to be much more convincing, given that he truly cared, and he was certainly not as hungover. Rawson would pull the thing together—what was left of it—in the final argument.

When Clark stepped down from the witness box, Mrs. Field, rose, took Clark firmly by the hand, and mother and child disappeared into the corridor outside the courtroom for a time. Bert figured the kid had to pee. Maybe they both did. Understandable.

P.O. Nobin outlined the defense. ... he had known the defendant and his family, and he knew that there must be some cause for the awful crime, and he would show that, while engaged in a little quarrel with the girl, he had struck her in self-defense and by accident had killed her. When he realized what he had done, he lost his reason entirely and completed the awful details of the crime. —Fergus Falls *Weekly Journal*, November 24, 1887.

Ingeborg Helle, Nels' Sister

Mrs. Hillen [Helle], who is trying so hard to help him, she is not of much aid to his counsel. She seems to be fairly intelligent, but when they placed her on the witness stand neither the counsel or the court could stop her loquaciousness. The prisoner's brother sat in the audience and did not venture near the prisoner. Mrs. Hillen (sic) - Nels is my youngest brother. He left home six years ago; he left very suddenly and we lost track of him for some time ...—Fergus Falls Weekly Journal, November 24, 1887.

The sun had started its path toward the horizon on this late November day. Streaks of melon-colored light splashed across the sky outside the courtroom, the musky scent of so many bodies seated in proximity mixed with the vague nuttiness of wood rubbed with linseed oil. Soft whispers circulated as a small woman with a thin face and a quick step took the oath and sat down. She didn't fidget, glance at the jury, or smooth her hair into place. She sat perfectly still, leaning slightly forward, anxious for P. R. Nobin's first question that would allow her to speak at last. Ingeborg Holong Helle had endured the testimony of the prosecution's witnesses in rigid silence, although seeing little Clark on the stand prompted a deluge of tears to cascade down her face. She couldn't help but think about the little brother who died in her care; this was a burden she still carried, even though she couldn't have been responsible for his illness.

"So, like little Peder, he seemed, though Peder's skin those last days had a rosy translucence to it—not like Clark's wind-burnished ruddy cheeks," she thought.

Ingeborg was just a teenager then, and she was terrified she'd lose Nels, too. She begged *Mor* to come and sit with him while she took over the cooking. Nels was a year younger than Peder, but he was a tough little *nisse*. That's what he looked like, she thought, with his sky-colored eyes, tiny ears, and perfect red circles on the apples of his cheeks. Not at all like this child, who sat before her in the witness box, with a wide face anchored on his blocky shoulders. This sturdy boy named Clark could never have succumbed to the fever that took one of her brothers and left the other a strange little creature.

Several years later Nels was leading a colt out from the pasture, she testified. A storm had come up suddenly and the colt was afraid. It had whirled around and kicked out with his back legs.

"It got him right in the head! We t'ought he'd die right d'ere! He's had terrible headaches since then, yah. And he don't like storms. He gets frightened. I don't tink he's ever been quite right," and she tapped her head several times with her index finger.

A rush of words, starting over from the first moments of little Nels' life, when she carried the tiny boy on a pillow, like her favorite doll. ... his illness (again), his difficulties with his lessons, when he finally got well enough to go to school ... the distance—always—on his sad little face ... On she went, muffling phrases through her handkerchief when she dabbed at her wet eyes and running nose. Nobin politely tried to bring it to an end; Lewis was not so polite, but no approach seemed able to turn off the torrent of information Ingeborg felt compelled to supply.

Until she turned to Judge Baxter and then the members of the jury, although they appeared unengaged by this time, and said, "So, then … you must see! He is not like you and me! *Gud hjelpe meg!*" and she finally took a deep breath. God must help me!

Baxter grabbed the moment of hesitation and ordered her to step down.

"You must not take his life!" she cried, taking a step toward the jury. Nobin gently took her arm and nudged her back to her seat.

Rasmus Bernager Testifies- Live in Ada; In 1885, July, Holong came to my house and wanted work; I hired him, agreeing to pay him $1 a day in haying $3 in harvesting and $1.50 in stacking; he acted very peculiar at times, seeming uneasy and restless; he would wander from one subject to another in his conversation; he seemed afraid of the elements and when he saw it clouding up he was afraid it would hail; his sleep was broken and at times he suffered from headaches. —Fergus Falls *Weekly Journal,* November 24, 1887.

Kittil Holong, Nels' Brother

"You see? You see?" Kittil was on his feet, shaking his finger at Rasmus Bernager, who was nervously repositioning himself in the witness chair. "My sister tells the truth! This is the way he is! Not so good," and Kittil, too, poked at his head with his finger.

Judge Baxter banged away with his gavel and shouted, "Sit down and be quiet!!

Kittil ignored it and shook his arms, palms toward the ceiling, shouting over the din of voices, quick to add a comment, "You must believe this, because it is the truth!"

More banging of the gavel, and finally Kittil straightened out his jacket, and sat down heavily on the bench closest to the back of the room. Bert had watched him take that spot the first day of the trial, too. He couldn't get much farther away from his brother. In fact, he wouldn't even sit with his sister. He sat on the end of the row, where he refused to move over for those who came later. It was enough to diminish even further what small regard the town had for this unsettling man's family.

"You will be respectful, Mr. Holong, or you will not be allowed in this courtroom!" the judge hollered back.

Nobin turned, shook his head at Kittil, and rose to face the bench. "There will be no further disruptions, Your Honor," he said.

But there would be. When Kittil showed up, there would be a disruption. Rawson knew the type. He and Nobin exchanged glances. "He's your friend, Pete," Bert said, leaning into his colleague. "Let's see you keep that promise."

At 10:30, the prisoner was placed on the stand. He staggered up and as soon as he was sworn hid his face. ... He was not on the stand to exceed ten minutes. —Fergus Falls *Weekly Journal,* November 24, 1887.

The Prisoner Testifies

Rawson stared at the single page of notes on the desk in front of him and muttered, "I told you this wouldn't work." It was meant for Nobin, who was earnestly trying to coax a few words from their client. Nels' arm was sprawled on the railing; his head was resting in the crook of his elbow. Sometimes he'd put his head up and rest his chin on his hand.

"I don't recall," he'd say, then bury his face again.

"Sure, now you don't recall," Bert thought with rising frustration. "Now's your chance to show these people just how much of an idiot you really are, and you can't recall!" It was like cajoling a five-year-old to eat his peas, and Nobin gave up.

Drs. Cole, Bedford and Reynolds then testified as to his mental condition. Dr. Cole said that he considered him almost an idiot, yet he

was intelligent enough to know the difference between right and wrong. —
Fergus Falls *Weekly Journal*, November 24, 1887.

Bert Rawson: A Verdict and a Whiskey

"Almost an idiot?" How is that different from "idiot?"
Knowing the difference between right and wrong? How
convenient! Bert was sure this was exactly the definition Baxter
and Lewis had in mind when they hired "good" doctors for
their "expert" opinions.

The trial was wrapping up—little more than twenty-four
hours since its beginning—with an equally predictable closing
argument by County Attorney Lewis, who conceded that Nels
was "peculiar," but this did not constitute a defense. More
predictably, he reiterated the need for the county to save face.

*Mr. Lewis made a strong speech and in closing asked the jury to render
a verdict such as would ensure the safety of our homes and to retrieve the
good name of Otter Tail County from the odium which had been fastened
upon it for its unpunished crimes. Judge Baxter then charged the jury. ...
He told them that premeditation did not have to exist even a moment in
the mind of the person committing the crime ... In regard to the prisoner
not being of sane mind he charged them that it must be proved beyond a
doubt by the defense. The charge on the whole was apt to create an
unfavorable view of the defendant's case.* —Fergus Falls *Weekly
Journal*, November 24, 1887.

Court was adjourned. Judge Baxter departed in haste for
home and supper with his wife. The good citizens of Fergus
Falls also rose to take their suppers in nearby saloons, if
possible, so as not to miss the jury's decision. They needn't
have worried about it; the chatter had barely dissipated, and
most observers had made it but a few feet from the courthouse
steps, when the announcement of a verdict came. Baxter was
fetched, the crowd poured back into the court room, Kittil sat
in his spot, stone-faced, while the ladies' skirts glided over his
knees and men's boots tripped over his own. Bert Rawson

skittered to his seat, the taste of a double whiskey still fresh in his mouth.

The Feeling Intense: *Until the conviction of Holong a murder had never been punished in Otter Tail County, and it had been the scene of many a bloody and cruel one, and on many instances there had been no doubt as to the guilty ones. Accordingly, when the news of Holong's capture and confession had become known the universal feeling was that he should never escape punishment, but all wanted the law to take its course. —* Fergus Falls *Weekly Journal*, April 18, 1888

Bert sat alone at the poker table in the back of The Mint. A bottle of rye was on another table within reach of him. He was spinning a shot glass, empty, in his right hand and turning the pages of the Fergus Falls *Weekly Journal* with his left. He knew Nettie was expecting him for supper, but he also knew that she wouldn't be at all surprised when he didn't show up. His ranting following the verdict was wearing on her and upsetting the children.

"Fifteen minutes, Nettie! Fifteen minutes to decide to hang the poor clod! Might have at least showed some decorum and let folks eat their goddam supper!"

"I'm going to feed Horace," she had answered and disappeared into the kitchen with baby Helen tucked in her right arm and Horace clutching the little finger of her left hand."

"Canting buggers! He shouted to no one from the front hall.

She was relieved to hear the door slam on his way out.

"That's what they are," he added as he stomped down the porch steps.

His card-playing pals wouldn't show up for a while. He had time to himself, which was a blessing—for everybody. He snapped the paper into a fold and flattened it on the table to read:

When Mr. Rawson arose to address the jury in behalf of the prisoner, he arose to a difficult task. There was absolutely no ground to stand on save that the prisoner was not of sound mind. He laid the greatest stress on the fact that since he was 6 years old, he had not been in full possession of his mental faculties. He said that for thirty years he had lived a passive life, doing nothing wrong and simply doing what others had told him. It did not seem possible that he could have been in his right mind when he did this awful deed. He did not expect an acquittal but asked for a verdict not more severe than murder in the second degree. —Fergus Falls *Weekly Journal*, November 24, 1887.

Underwood's paper was careful to *sound* principled in its rendition of Bert's closing argument. Fine. Bert considered it strictly a required formality anyway, along with the adherence to all procedures guided —and sure to be scrutinized—by state officials in St. Paul. He wouldn't doubt they planned to send a heated railcar up to transport the entire jury to the Winter Carnival in St. Paul in celebration of bringing our wayward county back into the state's fold.

There would be a hanging. He was certain. But not until an appeal. Nobin was already working on it. Rawson, however, had a more relaxed obligation. It was back to keeping the strings loose in town, so's a fella could play some cards and enjoy his whiskey in peace.

On the Thursday following Tuesday, on which he was convicted, the counsel argued for clemency. The court took the case under advisement and announced it would pass sentence at the opening of the court Friday after dinner. ... There were but a few present in the court room at this time, Judge Baxter not announcing when the sentence would be made as he did not desire any scene or unnecessary excitement. Holong's brother and sister, however, came in and insisted on staying in spite of the advice of the officers. ... When the judge was about to begin, he was commanded to stand up, which he did, but, as usual, he leaned his head on his elbow on the clerk's desk and gazed at the floor. —Fergus Falls *Weekly Journal*, April 19, 1888

Rawson had miraculously made it to court on time for the closing of his official duties in the State vs. Nels Olson Holong. Nobin was scribbling away again when Rawson pulled the seat out next to him.

"What the devil was there to scribble about?" Bert thought but couldn't be bothered with asking. He was revisiting, in his mind, the state's flip-flopping on a point of law critical to this case. Territorial law enacted mid-century required hanging for premeditated murder, but that didn't last long. Soon after the Rebellion, the law was changed to require a jury recommendation—and wouldn't you know it? Nobody hanged. In the early 80s, the decision (such as it was) flopped back to the bench, who controlled the only out: the "exceptional circumstances" clause. What, exactly, that meant, nobody knew, which gave a district court judge significant power to weigh the evidence using his own scale.

"Mayor" was becoming an ever-more attractive job title to Bert Rawson.

Baxter's full grey eyebrows were pinched together into one furry line across his forehead, and he was fairly spitting out the words written on a sheet of paper in front of him. He had prepared them with some conviction.

Your counsel claim that the court has the discretionary power to sentence you to imprisonment for life instead of pronouncing upon you the sentence of death. ... I should be glad to agree with them in this case, but am unable to do so. The exceptional circumstances which would justify the court in indicting upon you the lowest penalty—that of imprisonment for life—do not exist in this case. —Fergus Falls *Weekly Journal*, April 19, 1888

Baxter's speech to the condemned man—and Bert's musings about the often-fickle nature of what we called The Law—were interrupted by a Kittil outburst.

"But they do exist, they do!" he shouted. "This isn't a court of law! You are sacrificing a man because you must have a hanging! The State is pushing you, yah? I know dis! It's true! But dis is not justice!"

Kittil pronounced it "yoostice," but Bert quite agreed, no matter how you said it. Kittil's "loquacious" sister was more restrained, but her lined face and red eyes evidenced her more private struggle. Love … and profound grief. That's what Bert saw when she tilted her head away from Kittil and let her eyes rest again on the brother who had finally lifted his head from his arm. Kittil wasn't about to stop, but neither was Baxter. The courtroom was so raucous by this time that Bert figured he was the only one—besides the *Journal* reporter—who absorbed any of Judge Baxter's pronouncement.

You should not deceive yourself with the vain hope that any earthly power will interfere to stay the hand of the law or prevent the carrying out of the sentence about to be passed upon you, but should look for pardon and forgiveness only to Him that is the source of all power. —Fergus Falls *Weekly Journal*, April 19, 1888

Rawson half-expected Baxter to lead the little band of those present in the damn Lord's Prayer. "Separation of Church and State. It's in the Constitution, Baxter, you backwoods, gasbag," Bert thought. "And you can bet your ass that somebody will try his damndest to interfere! Very soon, Baxter, you're going to be dealing with a formidable earthly power just down the street—in the mayor's office!"

6. They Try to Save Him, November 23, 1887-April 12, 1888

veryone said 1887-88 was an especially mild winter, but to Ingeborg it was severe. Worse than Iowa. Colder, more snow and windier. Oh, the wind! As she valiantly went from house to house, farm to farm, town to town, saloon to saloon, she was fearless, talking to anyone kind enough to listen to her about what it means to hang someone!

She paused long enough to spend Christmas back in Decorah, Iowa, with her son Louis, *Mor* and *Far*. It was a somber holiday—a struggle to create a *God Jul* at all. There were candles on a tiny tree on Christmas Eve, and the church service was a huge relief for all: nothing to do but let the loving hand of God enfold this tortured family for a time. *Far* complimented *Mor* on the spareribs, as always, but struggled to eat enough to be at all convincing. Ingeborg asked Louis to put out some porridge for the *nisse*. At fifteen, he was not interested in child's play, but felt he had to go along. Nels had never got too old for this Christmas ritual and had been especially delighted when he could share it with his young nieces and nephews.

Louis stepped outside the kitchen door cradling the bowl of porridge in his rough, teenaged hands. His mother followed and touched his arm. She was captured by the moonshine glinting on the snow. How could there be such beauty at a time like this? He turned back to see her smiling at him, but when her gaze shifted to the North Star pointing with such finality to the place far away where her brother waited in a jail cell, the sadness again flickered in her tiny blue eyes. She wanted to give everyone hope, but she had only the smallest shred of hope herself. Louis walked to the shed and put the porridge right where the imaginary little creatures were sure to find it. If this small gesture eased his mother's suffering, he was most willing to do it.

Not long after the holidays, Ingeborg stood just inside the door of a modest frame house in Pelican Rapids. A little girl of ten or eleven answered the door and ran to the kitchen and quickly returned with her mother, who was drying her hands on an apron tied around her waist.

"*God dag,*" the mother said, and Ingeborg flushed with relief. Another Norwegian! She was bound to be sympathetic.

"*Jeg heter Fru Helle.* Nels Holong's …"

"*Ja, jeg vet det,*" the woman answered.

Everyone knew Ingeborg's name, and who her brother Kittel was. The word had spread quickly about the intrepid Norwegian woman and the petition, now several pages long with hundreds of signatures. A small bottle of ink and a pen wrapped in a cloth nestled in the small purse swinging from her wrist.

"*Kom, kom,*" the woman said, and motioned for Ingeborg to follow her into the kitchen. Norwegian or no, the parlor would be reserved for more appropriate guests here, as well. The woman poured coffee and offered her *fattigmann*. The irony of the "poor man" cookies was not lost on Ingeborg, but good manners demanded she accept the refreshments. She was now accustomed to the usual response of signing the petition she had carried with her around Otter Tail County in Minnesota and Winneshiek County in Iowa. Enough signatures and the Governor might stay Nels' impending execution. Oh, Lord God above! Please let this come to pass!

"No, I don't believe in hanging. It's not right, but what can I do? … What is going to happen to our county? … We have to do something, Mr. Underwood says."

Ah, yes. Mr. Underwood. She'd heard that he had bought out the *Telegram* and the *Democrat* (both of which didn't have enough of that political party to sustain them), so his newspaper, the Fergus Falls *Journal,* had a tight grip on what people read and heard—and what they believed. But another signature had to mean something … it just had to. So, on she went. More coffee sitting at many more kitchen tables, but just as frequently standing alongside a wagon, reaching with the petition and the pen toward another unfamiliar face, or waiting deferentially in a shop for a customer to complete her purchase before approaching the proprietor behind the counter. She knew that even if the shopkeeper was sympathetic, he was not about to admit it in front of anyone. Sometimes she got nothing more than a solemn look and a shake of the head. Not possible for this shopkeeper to associate his name with controversy, which was the case with many businessmen.

They Try to Save Him: *The sentence of death had scarcely been passed before a start was made to secure a commutation of his sentence to that of imprisonment for life. The basis was that he was an idiot. Despite the fact that the physicians who had examined him had testified as to his mental soundness and that the court and jury had unanimously passed upon the case the petition found ready signers and over 2,000 names were secured in this and in the county where he lived in Iowa. They seemed to forget his fearful crime and signed it as they sign everything else without knowing what it meant.* —Fergus Falls *Weekly Journal,* April 19, 1888

Jake the Jailor

Mrs. Helle and her brother were around and stopped by to see Nels regularly when they weren't traveling around the county collecting signatures on their petition to the Governor or grasping at similar straws with the vain hope their brother could be saved. In the meantime, it was Alonzo and Jake, his jailor, who got to know Nels best. Hard not to when Nels was always there.

It was a peculiar thing to Alonzo, whose wife's younger siblings and mother lived with them, so he knew what it was like to wake up every day to someone not your own kin. Eventually, though, they felt like family, particularly when Alice occasionally scolded her sister about scorching his shirt collars or the pillow slips. Then her mother would bicker with her over just how to stir the gravy and the whole business seemed so natural it made him feel more at home—like he had a family with children of his own.

181

Jake paused in his game of checkers with Nels. The condemned man stopped to roll a cig, which gave him time to scowl at the board and give the impression that he was strategizing his next move. Really, he was figuring out just what Jake had set up for him, in the interest of keeping the game going. Nels took pleasure in spotting these opportunities. Whether he understood how the game was supposed to be played was anybody's guess. At last, Nels would spot the sequence of jumps on the board, laboriously make his moves, and exclaim, "*Jeg har deg!*"

Jake would chuckle and say, "Yah, you got me again." The game would proceed for a few more manufactured moves, Jake would fold up the board and bag the checkers, give Alonzo a wink and drop the game back on the shelf.

"*Veldig godt, veldig godt,*" Nels would say, as he rolled another one. Very good. Just normal. Kind of like a family with a not very bright boy.

If they were lucky, Kittil wouldn't show up. Alonzo always felt like all the air got sucked out of the jail when Kittil was there, with nothing but the haze from Nels' constant smoking left to breathe. The *Journal* had even picked up on the general opinion circulating about Kittel. "He is a good deal more of an idiot than Nels and the authorities should take care of him before he does any harm," it had said. Alonzo didn't know how "the authorities" should "take care of him," but he was sure Underwood would bring up his little warning, should Kittil step over whatever "line" the paper had fabricated.

Mrs. Helle's visits—Ingeborg's—on the other hand, were less fraught with tension. Heavier with sorrow, the older lady giving herself no relief from her family's burden. But she did her best to be civil and to bring Nels whatever small comforts she could provide.

"Look Nels," she'd chirp. "I brought you some of Mors' *fattigmann* all the way from Decorah!"

"Yah?" Nels would say and take a bite of the crisp pastry.

"And *julekake!*"

Nels' eyes would sparkle a little and then lapse back into a faraway look.

"Nels?" she'd ask.

"Yah?"

"Try some." And he would. "*Er deg godt?*"

He'd take another bite. "*Veldig godt, veldig godt.*"

She'd almost imperceptibly turn her head from side to side. It wasn't exactly "no," but she was looking for something. "Nels?"

"Yah? … *Takk. Takk. Mange takk.*"

Her face softened. At least he remembered to say thank you, with her prompting. Like a child.

Sheriff Brandenburg: No Expectations

As impressed as one had to be that Mrs. Helle and Nels' sympathizers collected something around 2,000 signatures, the effort fell flat on its face. The sheriff didn't find it at all surprising that Nels' lawyers—or at least Nobin—still didn't give up, even after his sentencing. Nobody likes losing a high-profile case.

A final effort at an insanity defense was attempted with a direct appeal to Governor McGill. Alonzo expected nothing to change, as the state had no motivation to avoid a hanging. The Governor hadn't indicated otherwise from the outset, which could be seen as justifying the inevitable outcome: Otter Tail County had better get its house in order.

The Honorable Andrew R. MacGill, Governor, February 1888

The Governor was fed-up with the statewide talk about the dense Norwegian from Iowa—never mind the reputation of outlying counties for their capricious disregard for state law. "Probably they think we're not paying attention and don't care," the Governor could even now be muttering to his wife as he readied for bed, flinging his stiff collar on the dresser top in their bedroom. His wife simply watched, the covers tucked under her chin, as her husband snapped his suspenders off and sat, heavily, on the edge of the bed to remove his shoes.

"Otter Tail. Where is this God-forsaken place, anyway? It's been, what, a few years since they asked to be part of this state. They asked! Oh, but they want to make up their own rules, which sounds decent enough, but for all their damned exceptions. Seven, I've been told! Seven unpunished murders—*and* a lynching, Mary! A lynching! Get on with it, I say! That's what I told them. Take care of it! If those two doctors let him off ... well, I don't know what!"

He flung his trousers over the wooden valet, bounced onto his side, and jerked the quilt over his shoulders.

The Doctors Arrive in Secret, February 1888

Dr. Cyrus K. Bartlett and Dr. J.E. Bowers—called in by the Governor and completely new to the case—arrived on a sloppy, snowy day. Jake hung their heavy overcoats on the pegs behind the wood stove and offered them coffee from the pot steaming on the stove, which they accepted. Nels had no idea why they were there, but visitors he didn't know gave him another chance to share his side of the story, and if they'd tried to visit him, he figured they must be there to help him.

It wasn't the Sheriff's place to interfere. "These gentlemen would like to talk to you," the sheriff told him, and Nels nodded a little and sat down on the bed. Jake brought in a couple of chairs for the doctors, who sat facing Nels. They were very well dressed. Nels would behave and not rant about the Fields. It was easy enough for Sheriff Brandenburg to hear at least bits and pieces of their conversation.

"You understand what you did?"

This was a trick question. Did they not see the blank stare? Brandenburg didn't even have to look; he'd seen it so many times.

"What does the law in this state say about homicide?"

The hesitation in answering questions. It wasn't that he wouldn't answer; he'd answered hundreds of questions—and truthfully! But he doesn't always understand you! Brandenburg felt like screaming, it was so painfully obvious. He speaks Norwegian, given the opportunity. Did you notice?

"Now, Nels, you need to tell us what you know. Do you understand? You know that it was wrong, don't you?"

Nels, ever ready to please, answered.

"Yah, yah. It vas da wrong ting I did, yah."

You know that it's wrong to kill another person, don't you?"

Did they miss the flicker of anger in his eyes? The fidgeting?

"How old are you, Nels? Do you know how old you are?"

Did they not hear that their tone became progressively more tuned to questioning a child?

Can you read? Will you read this?

"Det er Bibelen." (The Bible.)

Nels was raised in the church and confirmed. His father, Mrs. Helle had shared, had helped to establish the Lutheran church in Madison County, Iowa. Even if he couldn't read it in English, if he had a few cues, he could tell them—close enough—what it said. He even had a Norwegian Bible in his cell! Well, they probably wouldn't notice that either.

"Ah, yes … indeed it is. You do understand, don't you."

That was a statement, not a question. Nels had fooled 'em again. There was one thing at which he had become accomplished: convincing people that he understood—that he was all right. Do you see? No! You may very well have a clear dictum not to see.

These thoughts Brandenburg shared with no one, although he had let a couple of comments slip in front of his wife, Alice. "Such an idiot … He doesn't really …" He had his back to Alice, but she caught the tone in his voice.

"You don't think …?" she said with a little gasp, and rushed to turn him toward her, hoping to catch the answer in his eyes. He just wobbled his head and turned his back again. It was barely a "no."

Alonzo Brandenburg sensed more than he was willing to say. He has seen Nels rolling his cigs', pissing in the pot under the bed, slurping the coffee with cream in the bowl he holds in

185

both hands. He's heard him win at checkers when he had no idea how to win, hold surprisingly coherent conversations with the crazy guy in the next cell, and bawl like an orphaned calf when the poor man was shipped off to the insane asylum at St. Peter.

Nels could remember details about his entire life that stunned Jake and Alonzo, but Nels' renditions had the ring of oft repeated stories. Practiced. He worked at it. It was the way he got by in life. None of what he said was definitive evidence, but if you put it all together … Alonzo was plagued by wonderment. Idiot? Guess not, no. Insane? Temporarily perhaps, at that moment with Lillie. Maybe.

As usual, Nels hadn't been the least bit crafty or manipulative. But, as Alonzo now saw, the doctors were. …

While there is some eccentricity of character, there is not, to our minds, any tangible evidence of imbecility or insanity in the said Nels Olson Holong.

Very respectfully submitted,

Cyrus K. Bartlett, M.D.

J.E. Bowers, M.E.

The Day Is Set: *The governor at once decided not to interfere with the verdict of the court and jury, and to prevent any further suspense or efforts by his friends, at once issued the death warrant authorizing his execution on Friday, April 13 … Holong was told who the two men were who had visited him and became quite despondent, evidently because he had talked so freely with them.* —Fergus Falls *Weekly Journal*, April 19, 1888

Bert Rawson: Let's Get This Over With, April 10, 1888

Of course, the governor didn't interfere; the governor got exactly what he'd intended, but Bert Rawson had no time to think about another stab at a sentence reprieve for Holong. At the time, he was too busy with his own political career. Then, right before the local election April 3, some random Minneapolis lawyer (the whole state was following the case by this time) found discretionary verbiage in a state statute that was floated as a last-ditch effort to save Holong's life over a technicality. It would take an appeal to the Minnesota Supreme Court, but the Supreme Court wasn't going to buy it; Bert would've bet his own life on that.

State v. Holong, State of Minnesota vs. Nels O. Holong
Minnesota Supreme Court
Decided April 30, 1888
H. E. Day, Thomas Canty, and P. 0. Noben, for the motion
M. E. Clapp, Attorney General, against the motion

On the 4th day of April inst., the defendant appealed from the judgment to this court, and now moves the court for a stay of execution pending the appeal. On the motion his counsel states the grounds on which the appeal is taken, which are that the indictment is insufficient to justify a conviction for murder in the first degree; that the statute which authorized the governor, in capital cases, to cause execution to be done by issuing his warrant for that purpose, has been repealed by the Criminal Code. If we entertained any doubt on either of these propositions, we would not hesitate, in so grave a case, to stay execution until they could be fully and formally argued and determined in this court. But the propositions are entirely groundless.

Never mind. By that time, Bert Rawson was busy celebrating his impressive win that placed him decisively in the mayor's office. His appeal to unite Republicans and Democrats was not completely ingenuous. "I owe my election to the Republicans, to the working men—to all except the prohibitionists," he'd announced in his victory speech. He hated the prohibitionists, men for whom he had no sympathy or respect, and he said so.

187

Benjamin Underwood, publisher of the Fergus Falls *Journal*, was standing across from the courthouse, looking irritatingly perfect in a new suit. Bert had seen it in a store window just last week and recognized it from an ad in Underwood's paper. "Worked a deal, I s'pose," Bert said to Jake's nag tied in front of the Court House. The horse scratched his face on Bert's coat sleeve, leaving a mass of shedding winter hair. It was hardly a new suit, but the horse got a rap on the nose anyway.

Underwood was rocking back and forth on his feet—heels, toes, heels, toes—and fiddling with a cigar maintained a fraction of an inch from his mouth, so he could grab a puff when he paused long enough to let one of the other boys opine yet another rendition of the tremendous job everyone had done to bring about law and order in this town. The hearty guffaws that accompanied their elucidations sent the smoke zipping in little swirls in complete disorder around the men. Ass lickers.

"You boys are going to have to miss it, the way it looks," Underwood said, and jerked his thumb over his shoulder in the direction of the jail, where the pounding continued. "Brandenburg ain't budging on that. Don't even know 'xactly when, do I? You ask me, I think the whole town deserves to be there, what with the affair such a trauma, of course. But I don't tell the law what to do, now do I?"

The men nodded and mumbled an affirmation.

"*No, technically, he didn't tell the law what to do,*" Bert thought. "*But he sure as hell found ways to have an impact.*"

Overall, though, Underwood was squeaky clean, which made him so annoying. The fact that he was a Republican just made it worse. At least Benjamin's father, A.J. Underwood could be said to have faults. Rawson had his public beefs with A.J., but he secretly liked the man, and was saddened when he died suddenly a couple of years back. Now the lot of 'em— Brandenburg, Underwood and the rest of those Republicans— had a self-righteous streak that irked Bert Rawson to no end. Not nearly as obnoxious as the prohibitionists, but that group was still licking their wounds after a trouncing in their one-issue mayoral campaign.

Rawson's card-playing pals were refreshing, by comparison: mouthy, irreverent, loose, you might say. The quarrels they had with the local authorities—and by association, Underwood's newspaper—were subjects for jokes, not anger, provoking gales of laughter in the telling and retelling of their minor, but frequent, scrapes with the law, all having to do with a man's right to relax with a few drinks and a friendly game of chance. Hell, it was hard to get worked about any of it anymore, though. Things were going to be different now that Bert Rawson was the mayor.

7. All Is Over, April 13, 1888

T he wall blocking off the site of the execution was nearly complete and the work of building the scaffold itself was just underway. Sheriff Brandenburg paused in his supervisory duties long enough to retreat to his office, get a cup of coffee and talk himself down—once again—from the emotional precipice that inched closer, as Friday, April 13 loomed.

Loud guffaws drew his attention out the window toward a group of men—Alonzo knew them all. The mood in town had been a little too celebratory for Brandenburg since Holong's final effort at a reprieve had failed, and he didn't have to hear the rest of it, since he'd already heard it all. The men threw their heads back, mouths open in uproarious laughter. Alonzo shut the window.

Maybe they weren't even talking about the hanging; maybe they had moved on. But for Brandenburg, it had a sinister quality. They were not the ones who would have to pull that lever. The sheriff turned to the coil of rope on the floor in the corner behind his desk. Italian hemp, he was told, and it wouldn't stretch. He had witnessed this himself on that morning in Duluth, which had the only execution in the state since the death penalty was restored. Can't use just any rope, so it was simpler and cheaper to use the same one.

He picked up the rope. About the color of a lamp wick, it was. He'd stretch it anyway … not about to take chances on screwing this up. God, he had to think about something else!

He turned his attention to accounts. The hanging cost plenty, about $2,500, what with keeping the jail open and heated all winter just for one prisoner, most of the time. The death watch: two men at three dollars apiece per day. The scaffolding alone amounted to a lot of lumber. Nels' board at the jail. Jake's hours.

Jake was good to Nels and Nels had asked a reporter to place a "thankful card" in the Journal, for "mostly Jake," Nels had said. Jake could afford the kindnesses he gave and allow a relationship with their prisoner. He didn't have to pull that lever, either. For that, the sheriff would be paid $500, same as the St. Louis County sheriff when he hanged the guy in Duluth. He slammed the ledger book shut, tossed it into the desk drawer and spun his chair around to again face the rope coiled in the corner. It looked like a snake. Threatening. He tossed the canvas wood carrier over it, half expecting it to retaliate and strike.

... Holong asked the sheriff if he had not been good since he had been in jail, and the sheriff said he had. Holong said the officers had treated him well. The sheriff asked him if there was anything he wanted, adding if there was, he would get it for him. Holong said not but added he would like some fresh fish and tomatoes for supper. He then told Sheriff Brandenburg that he hoped to meet him on the other side... His breakfast was brought in. It was a whole roast chicken, some tomatoes and bread and butter. He said he was pretty hungry, and the way he ate would not have led anyone to think that it was his last breakfast on earth ... The watch asked him what he wanted for dinner. He replied that he was going to dine with Jesus ... At 1:30 the ministers entered Holong's cell and remained with him until 1:45, when the sheriff entered accompanied by the death watch. "Nels, the time has come to do my duty," said he. ... He was taken into the corridor where he asked the sheriff to fix the handcuffs which hurt his hand. The sheriff did it and asked him if it was all right. ... Pastor Wold offered a prayer in Norwegian. —Fergus Falls *Weekly Journal*, April 19, 1888.

"Be a man, Nels," the sheriff said when the noose rested around Nels' neck, but he immediately regretted the useless directive. His nervous hands pulled the lever harder than was necessary, and he immediately descended the platform and strode toward the privacy of his office. A wave of nausea engulfed him as he reached the door. He slammed it behind him and collapsed in his desk chair.

He missed seeing the black cap slipping aside a little for a momentary glance at the face underneath, its veins swollen to

192

bursting and the tongue lulling out. He had no interest in observing the half a dozen convulsive quivers of the legs—hardly strong enough to be called kicks—and the obscene stillness that followed. There would be a pulse for a few minutes—eleven and a half minutes someone found it necessary to tell him later.

The aroma of roast chicken mixed with that of oily fish, and Alonzo glanced down at the sardine tin in the waste bin. He had no words, no understanding of what he felt. Something like the day that he and Alice had buried their tiny baby. That was unbearable to think of, so he rose and found himself walking to the empty cell. It wasn't good, but it was better. Cigarette butts. Lots of them in the can with rust around its edges. The daily calendar still hung on the wall. The Bible verses in Norwegian, one for each day, had been duly ripped off, one by one, and stopped on today's date, Friday the 13th. The checkerboard had remained in the corner. He jumped three of Nels' checkers—the red ones—but left them on the board, just as Jake had. Everyone who has a tender heart suffers for it.

Brandenburg didn't need to keep this job any longer. He was a director at the bank. There could be a larger future for him there, but at the moment, the decision was not so clear. He would have to run for re-election, and he would never face this task again, a thought that brought him a tiny bit of relief—enough to endure the noise of the county's grim task coming to completion—muffled voices, boots on hollow boards, a last thud—just beyond his closed door.

ALL IS OVER: THE LAST ACT IN THE FIELD—HOLONG TRAGEDY IS FINISHED. THE MURDERER SWUNG INTO ETERNITY AT THE JAIL AT 2 P.M.

THE TRAP IS SPRUNG AND THE CULPRIT PAYS THE PENALTY OF HIS MOST FIENDISH CRIME.

HE ATE WELL AND SLEPT SOUNDLY IN THE FACE OF HIS SOLEMN AND AWFUL DOOM.

THE STORY OF HIS BRUTAL MURDER RETOLD—
HISTORY OF THE CAPTURE AND TRIAL.

HE MAKES A STATEMENT BEFORE THE EXECUTION
GIVING THE DETAILS OF THE MURDER.

DESCRIPTION OF THE SCAFFOLD—THE ROPE—THE
DEADLY NOOSE—THE PARTICIPANTS.

It's Your Farm Now, Lillie

Mother had, despite her many ailments, found the energy to start spring cleaning early. Cleaning had become her passion; it was the one thing that steadied her. But it also exhausted her and frequently sent her to her bed to recuperate. She was on her hands and knees scrubbing out the bottom of the pantry cupboard, pans clattering as she stacked them on the table. Charles couldn't bear the din, nor could he watch her frantic work anymore. Everything jangled him, and he thought the damp chill of the afternoon might cool his churning discomfort. He grabbed his coat off the peg by the door and headed out.

It had rained early that morning, but the wind had shifted, and the clouds were racing across the sky to the southeast. He had managed to avoid the spot where he found Lillie last May. But now, on the day of her killer's execution, he thought it was time and he headed for the grove.

Mother called from the doorway, "Are you going back to Pomme de Terre?"

"No, Mother." He turned to face her. He had nothing more to say.

She looked past him, cocked her head toward the grove, got no response from Charles and went back inside.

That morning ... less than one year ago when he went to town with Mother ... Nels was just sort of lurking by the barn, watching Lillie, but he always looked so awkward that Charles took little notice. At least he was at the barn and looked to be ready for chores.

"I'm not staying here with that Mr. Holong!" she'd said.

The spot where Charles had found her was already sprouting prairie grasses. He couldn't imagine how anything could ever grow there again, but it was. A shred of her dress ... or was it her apron? ... matted with blood, mud, and pig manure, clung to a naked willow branch wedged in last year's dead grass. He broke off the branch and carried it toward the lake. Even the noise of his feet rustling in the thick grasses set his nerves on edge. He was relieved to stop at the sandy shore, where he plopped down on a large rock, still clutching the piece of willow.

"Well, Lillie, it's over," he said, and tapped the stick on the rock. But it wasn't over. The image of Lillie chasing the wagon's dust was as vivid as the day they'd left her. "Don't leave me here! Don't leave me!" she screamed. He had heard her husky voice in his head a thousand times a day ever since. "Don't leave me!"

He was going to leave her, though, and go back to Pomme de Terre. Maybe then the voice would fade, and the memory of his sister would be tolerable. Mother could stay here, rent out the acreage and sell most of the livestock.

"Sorry, Lillie. This is your farm now," he told her, and threw the willow branch as far as he could out into the deep blue green of the little lake.

... For the first time in the history of Otter Tail County a murderer has paid the penalty of his crime. ... His fate should be a warning that a murderer may come to grief in Otter Tail county, even if one never has in the past. —Fergus Falls *Weekly Journal*, April 19, 1888.

8. Lillie's Ghost

t Lillie's prodding, my odyssey took me back to the farm I had visited some twenty years earlier. I was trespassing again, but this time I was alone in the soundless, wooded hollow. I would have liked to stand on the edge of the little lake, now a Waterfowl Production Area, where Nels had sat and waited, and where Charles said goodbye to Lillie at last. But it was too late in the day to venture that far from the road, and I couldn't even see the lake. Whole forests can be cut down and grow again in a century. So, I sat nearby.

They say, those who believe, that ghosts stay around because of a wrong that was not made right, haunting the place where they died until there is a reason to stop. From what I understand, ghosts are unpredictable in their manifestations. If I believe any of it, it would be that. I never saw Lillie, and she didn't move things around or make spooky noises. She just wouldn't stay out of my head. Willful, that's what Lillie was. She'd made me traipse around Otter Tail County—driving down a gravel road that ended in a field, staring across a housing subdivision where a pioneer farm once stood, scrolling through piles of microfilmed newspapers in the county museum's library, wandering through cemeteries to read mossy tombstones, and so forth, and so on. Lillie would not let me stop. Impressive for someone who was … just what? A presence.

I made a lot of new acquaintances from the past in my research. Some I liked very much; some I wasn't sure what to think. I was struck, though, by the absence of true evil. Anywhere. Some suffered from illnesses, others made horrible choices. Judges and juries reflected the culture's interpretation of right and wrong. Not everyone agreed, but the system lurched forward.

I turned towards the western horizon to watch the deep blues and oranges melting together and cement my sense of direction. In late spring, this part of the country is treated to long sunsets with ribbons of colors shifting and becoming more spectacular until they finally dissolve into the earth's edge. This is when the hollow with the rock remains of a foundation took on a pale charcoal cast that was crawling up the hillside as fast as the sky crossed over into night.

I should have gone right then, while I could still see to pick my way through the deadfall a little better, but I didn't. I sat and waited for something to happen, just like I had years before. I did not see or even imagine a girl in white floating above the hollow. That didn't happen. But I did imagine that I heard the barely perceptible rustle of a wool skirt folding on the ground next to me, and I surely imagined that I heard a girlish sigh float up.

"Hello, Lillie," I said. "And goodbye, too. It's time to leave."

I sighed too. Leaves, still left on the oaks from last fall, crackled. We sat together and watched one take a leisurely dive to the ground, where it balanced on a broken branch, then tipped off onto the ground. But I suppose we couldn't wait and watch them all fall. I stood up.

This time, when I returned to the gravel approach off the county road, I knew I had left Lillie and her story at last. I wasn't sad about that, and if Lillie really was a present spirit, watching the oak leaf fall, I don't think Lillie was sad, either.

The click of the car door jolted me. I started it but turned the lights off. Lillie should be able to leave at last with the privacy of darkness. No more intrusions. A few stars were popping through the breaks in the clouds, and the moon had risen. These would guide me down the gravel road far enough to give her that.

THE OUTCOME

One could logically argue that Holong's defense failed because the crime was so horrific and the victim so young, but there were other forces at play. While it's true that Holong thoroughly incriminated himself, and he didn't meet the benchmarks for an insanity defense, this case wasn't just about Holong or his victim. It was the end game for a string of questionable verdicts.

The newspaper reports, the comments by the prosecution during Holong's trial, and the decision by the Governor himself all point to this: the county needed a hanging. There was a lot at stake in the larger picture, and the life of this migrant farmhand didn't much matter to the decision-makers. They had to establish law and order—or the appearance of it. They believed that their status as a county of the state of Minnesota and their ability to prosper depended on it.

An Insanity Plea

Medical science today has some comprehension of the continuum on which brain function exists and the complexities in describing normal function versus abnormal. But in 1887, from a legal standpoint, a person was either sane or insane, an idiot or not an idiot.

The legal basis for insanity was codified into British law in the mid-19th Century with the M'naughten Rule, which is still used in a majority of U.S. states, including Minnesota. It says that the defendant either did not understand what he or she did or failed to distinguish right from wrong, because of a "disease of mind." An "idiot," was a person with a severe intellectual disability, believed to have no chance of improvement.

To support an insanity claim, Nels Holong's sister Ingeborg testified about his childhood illness and an accident with a horse at about age twelve. Today's doctors tell us that a high fever, per se, in a child will not cause brain damage. However, there are severe or prolonged illnesses that can. Viral meningitis, for example, was a common affliction among children at the time and can cause disabilities. It's just as likely that he already had a problem with reading and missing a lot of school because of illness exacerbated it. References to his poor reading skills, as well as his good memory—so good that it surprised people, and they remarked about it—fit this profile. People who don't read well are often good aural learners, compensating by remembering details they've heard quite proficiently. This sheds no light, however, on the violence Nels used to kill and mutilate Lillie Field. But a brain injury could.

Nobody recognized precisely what was wrong with Nels, but they knew something was amiss. Holong freely shared the story about the horse with his jailer during his incarceration. The way he remembers it, he was twelve years old, leading two horses out of the pasture. A full-grown horse, especially a large, draft horse, can kill an adult with a well-placed kick; a twelve-year-old whose brain is still developing could certainly suffer permanent damage. Did he rest a sufficient length of time for a concussion, which he must have had, or was he sent right back to his chores as soon as he appeared able?

The U.S. National Institutes of Health says that traumatic brain injuries can lead to "personality changes, emotional or behavioral dysregulations, and persistent cognitive deficits." Among the possible behavior and emotional changes, the Mayo Clinic includes difficulty with self-control, difficulty in social situations, mood swings, lack of empathy for others, anger, and insomnia.

If this accident added to Holong's disability, he could have had a serious closed head injury that caused permanent damage.

Louisa Kjosa, the wife of Ted Kjosa, a descendant of the Holongs who lived near Decorah, Iowa, said in a telephone interview that his family today doesn't know why he left home. That information was never shared in family circles over the decades. (As many a Norwegian Lutheran will attest, stoic silence is considered the appropriate response to sensitive or uncomfortable personal issues.) There may have been worrisome behaviors, although it was reported that he "had done nothing wrong" for thirty years. But what constituted doing something wrong? Scraps with other men or behavior that made girls uncomfortable were not taken seriously, so did Holong's "peculiarities" cross the line for his respectable family?

Even so, it's hard to comprehend how he just disintegrated psychologically when he felt trapped in an emotionally confusing environment on the Field's farm that May morning in 1887. There had to have been a disconnect with reality when his ability to comprehend his actions was impaired, if not altogether absent. Still, he remembered it.

A Second-Degree Murder Plea

Besides his special needs as a brain-damaged adult and his inability to fully understand the ramifications of his actions, there were indications that the murder was not premeditated, but the fact that he had "come on" to Lillie likely was. He made no secret of his interest in her. But there is no straightforward evidence of an intention to hurt her, much less kill her. He wanted to court her, but lacked the skills to do it, and most certainly lacked the wherewithal to diffuse the escalating interchange in the Field's kitchen.

The prosecution claims it was Holong, not Lillie, who told Clark to return a shovel to the neighbors and called it evidence of premeditation. If that's so, how much time constitutes "premeditation?" A day? A minute? At what point would it become a crime of passion?

Premeditation, as it turns out, is no easier to pin down, legally, than an insanity plea. According to various sources, the amount of time necessary between the planning and the act to prove premeditation is determined on a case-by-case basis and requires only that the killing is intentional, deliberate and is carried out after prior consideration. But the duration of that period of consideration is not fixed by law.

To establish this crucial point in Holong's case, the prosecution put a six-year-old on the witness stand. Not that it mattered. In his instructions to the jury at the end of the trial, Judge Baxter shaved this finer point to the level of imperceptible. "Premeditation did not have to exist even a moment in the mind of the person committing the crime," he said. If Lillie had told Clark to return the shovel, as Nels claimed, Judge Baxter must have felt it necessary to offer his legal interpretation. But Holong still had a credible defense that could have saved his life.

Self-incrimination

Holong was the perfect fall guy for the county's law enforcement slippages, and he played right into their hands, professing his guilt, even correcting information about the crime and its aftermath with childlike persistence. At no time did he deny the events as he first told them, change his story in any substantive way, or spin his narrative to better support efforts on his behalf.

Holong could not have grasped the inevitability of what he was facing, or why would he have been so forthcoming, providing details that only he could know? Any prudent criminal would have denied the whole thing and said nothing or would have had his attorney plea bargain—a confession of second-degree murder for a prison sentence, rather than hanging.

But not Holong. Instead, he told the truth, just as he was taught at home and at church. The irony is that law enforcement would have had little more than Lillie's body to go on, but for Holong's telling (and retelling) of the crime.

It was also suggested that he had sexually assaulted her, which he denied. In fact, it would have been out of character for Holong to leave out the assault, if there was one, evidenced by his unwavering truth-telling. Not that it would have affected the outcome; his situation couldn't get any worse.

Not Crazy Enough

Behavior abnormalities in this era were all lumped together with little knowledge about the nuances possible and, although everyone agreed that Holong was not "normal," he wasn't "crazy" enough or enough of "an idiot" to slide neatly into the profile for an insane perpetrator, and he simply fell through the cracks of the social system, the legal system and the medical system. Six doctors had examined him and made their determinations, but, of course, all six were working off the same criteria. One, Dr. Cole, testified that he was "almost an idiot" but he knew right from wrong—and that was a critical point.

A means for assessing "idiocy" was the inability to carry on a coherent conversation, but of this, Holong was quite capable. He had been raised in a family of older siblings by parents who were connected to the founders of the Lutheran church in America. He certainly heard conversations involving sophisticated vocabulary on theology, politics, government, and social issues. These discussions were in Norwegian, however, and his examination and the trial were in English.

But Holong could speak and understand English—if the topics were familiar to him. But where would he have acquired the vocabulary to talk about his own mental capacity or the complexities of his case? He wouldn't have conversed about these topics in Norwegian, much less in English.

For all those times he didn't understand, or didn't have the vocabulary to respond, he could fall back on a near lifetime of trying to convince those around him that he was normal and that he fit in. It would have taken considerable effort to cover up what he himself could not fully understand. Even so, the consensus was that he was "not right in the head." Try as he might, he was not successful in convincing people that he was just like them.

He also knew that people who couldn't speak English very well were a step lower in the social strata than "real Americans" who spoke English as a first language. Add to this an austere Lutheran upbringing—to honor authority and to do as he was told—and he responded as he was taught, with cooperation, even if he didn't always know the implications of what he was saying.

It's hard to fathom how the expert doctors who examined him could not see his limited ability to understand, but there was yet another dynamic. The doctors who examined him were about as high profile as they could get in the state at the time. Brought in from Minnesota "insane asylums" by the Court, their reputations could be at stake. Minnesota was a young state; it couldn't have had many doctors with this kind of expertise, trusted to make what amounted to a life and death decision. They may very well have been among those setting the criteria they used to evaluate Holong. Were they "backed into a corner," in a sense, forced to follow their own rules?

Still, Holong should never have been facing the death penalty. The law allowed for life imprisonment or hospitalization for an insanity ruling. They were able to forge new territory with that recommendation, but once again, Holong fell through the cracks. The time had not yet arrived for a breakthrough decision that could have saved his life.

The County Needed a Hanging

Nels Holong hardly resembled a stereotypical murderer, and hanging him was, in fact, going to do nothing to contain violence in the county. Why the guilty ones in previous cases were acquitted and Holong became the perfect scapegoat is partly just miserable timing.

But that's an over-simplification. This county was in trouble for letting crime have its way so close on the heels of its establishment as a Minnesota county in 1872. Loose law enforcement may have been part of the landscape in newly settled territory, but a proper county was expected to play by *the state's* rules. The Fergus Falls *Journal* continued to do its part in hammering away at this message.

The newspaper's extensive report following the hanging also said, "His fate should be a warning that a murderer may come to grief" in Otter Tail County, "even if one never has in the past." It seems a bit overblown for the news report to boast that the county was now suddenly capable of bringing a murderer "to grief" because it was able to apprehend a special needs man (without incident), who told them everything with little provocation. Holong had fled on foot a few miles, stayed in the house he'd lived in recently, and visited a friend, who others in the area would surely have known was his friend. Justice will heretofore be done, based on the county's ability to apprehend this man? Seems a bit ludicrous, but if the *Journal* kept saying it, enough people would believe it, and that's all the county really needed.

Although everything possible had been tried and had failed, Holong's supporters still did not give up. Following his conviction, a petition that had been circulated in an effort to save him from being hanged had more than 2,000 signatures, which was close to ten percent of the population in Otter Tail County in 1888. The logistics of getting that many signatures were daunting, requiring considerable dedication, given the time, expense, inconvenience and even dangers associated with traveling in late winter and early spring.

Yet, the *Journal* was scornful. "They seemed to forget his fearful crime and signed it as they signed everything else without knowing what it meant," the newspaper said.

Unfortunately, the *Journal* did not see fit to print the petition (although it printed the statement by the doctors), and no copies or pieces of it exist, so there is no record of exactly what it said or who signed it, which might have been even more revealing. Were influential people among the signers? Perhaps not, or the *Journal* might have been more favorably impressed.

The local newspaper, law enforcement and the influential in the county made up their minds when

Holong was apprehended. With a mixture of relief and the expected vindication, they were "saved." But Holong was doomed.

Acknowledgments

I owe a great deal to the staff at the Otter Tail County Historical Museum, and in particular research assistant Vicky Anderson, who always seemed to know exactly where to find what I needed. Volunteers and staff at the History Museum of East Otter Tail County also came to my rescue. I found excellent support at the Wadena County Historical Society, the Douglas County Historical Society, and from Julie Drouillard for court records in the Otter Tail County Courthouse.

The Gale Family Library at the Minnesota History Center houses the original documents from the cases referenced in this book. The staff there were so efficient, locating for me the very indictments, coroner's reports, jury verdicts and other official business—most of it handwritten. Thrilling!

Peter Jannett, Research Analyst with the State Court Administrator's Office sent me to Tim Post at Mitchell-Hamline Law School, who connected me with Douglas Heidenreich, who was a storehouse of information on self-defense, laws regarding intoxication and felony crimes, the insanity defense, and many related issues.

Knowing an expert in genealogical research was also enormously helpful, and I thank Pam Berven for solving genealogy problems that enriched the stories. My thanks to readers along the way, including Pam, Martha Vetter, Tim Andersen and Margi Preus, for their careful insights.

My colleagues in the Minneapolis Writers Workshop heard various renditions of most of the book over a long period of time. Special thanks to Marlys, Mary, Denise, Jon Ivan, David, and Cynthia, who heard my initial essay "Lillie's Ghost" and said, "You have to write this book." So, I did.

About the Author

Janet Preus is a playwright, songwriter, lyricist, a writer and editor who lives on a lake in northern Minnesota. She's blended a life of teaching and directing theater with journalism, including as a reporter for an Otter Tail County radio station and news editor for the Fergus Falls *Daily Journal*. She has personal essays, a musical, a series of children's books, and many magazine articles and theater reviews published, has released recordings of original songs, and has won awards in journalism, nonfiction, playwrighting and songwriting. When not writing—with pencil on paper—she may be hiking or skiing in the woods with her dog Winter or cajoling her guitar-playing life partner to accompany her songs for an upcoming gig. "The 13th Crime" is her first book.

Endnotes

---

[i] The *St. Paul Dispatch* wrote following Erwin's death *"... the greatest criminal lawyer the Northwest ever knew [meaning the Midwest] ... an orator equaled by none, perhaps, except Ignatius Donnelly [Minnesota writer, orator and social reformer] ... he was in some respects the greatest intellect that ever shed its luster upon a Minnesota community."* Ramsey County *History, vol. 42, Number 4. Winter 2008.*

[ii] Town should be understood to mean "township," as distinguished in the newspapers of the time from village or city.

[iii] Because the pages were defective on the original hard copy, the exact date could not be read.

[iv] A common name for a German at the time.

[v] "Swamp," in Polish, is intended figuratively but can also be taken literally as the house sat on a small lake or pond, which, due to its size, could literally be called a slough—or swamp.

[vi] Defective original copy. Some words could not be read.

www.ingramcontent.com/pod-product-compliance
Lightning Source LLC
Chambersburg PA
CBHW030517020726
47494CB00004B/1130